The Cartwright Gardens Murder

By
J.S. Fletcher

We are pleased to present this easier-to-read,
specially formatted Classic Mystery Story,
The Cartwright Gardens Murder, by J.S. Fletcher
For your Reading Pleasure

Copyright © 2023
All Rights Reserved

Originally Published in 1924
This Edition Published in 2023

ISBN: 9798374594041

Chapter 1

Cartwright Gardens lies in the far east corner of Bloomsbury, somewhat south of the dreary Euston Road, and somewhat north of the still drearier quarter that fringes on the western confines of Clerkenwell. Whoever knows nothing of it and goes on a voyage of discovery must not expect what the name, taken literally, would seem to suggest...here are neither bushes nor brakes, flowers nor fruits.

What is here is a drab and dismal crescent of houses, fronted by an enclosure wherein soot and grime descend on the London plane tree and the London turf; an oasis, perhaps, in the surrounding wilderness of shabby streets, but only, as things go, for the brave sparrow and his restless stalker, the lodging-house cat. Maybe the place has seen better days; in these it presents a frontage of mean houses, in each of which it is all Lombard Street to a China orange that you would find, if not more families than one, at any rate a lodger or lodgers in addition to the nominal tenant. The houses look as if they accommodated lodgers; the men who come out of them early of a morning look as if they were lodgers; the women, who, at one hour of the day or another, stand at the doors, to traffic with wandering greengrocers or itinerant fishmongers, look as if they lived by letting lodgings.

And the young man who saw a certain extraordinary thing in Cartwright Gardens, at precisely fifteen minutes before midnight, on Monday, October 25th, 1920, was a lodger, and he saw it because, being a bit of a rhymster, he had been sitting up late to write verses, and, to cool his brow, had, at the moment mentioned, opened the window of his room, on the top floor of No. 85, and thrust head and shoulders into the silence of the autumn night. The name of this young man was Albert Jennison, and by calling he was a clerk. He was at this time one and twenty years of age, and he had been a clerk for four years, and, as far as he could see, he was going to be a clerk for ever. There were clerk-ships and clerk-ships; Jennison's job was lowish down in that scale. Its scene was a warehouse...dry goods...in the Gresham Street district of the city: he was in that warehouse, adding and subtracting, from nine o'clock in the morning until five o'clock in the afternoon. He had begun, at seventeen, at a pound a week: now he got three pounds ten, and his relations, who lived in the country and thought rustically, told him that he ought to consider himself well off, and that when he attained to just double his present stipend he would be a gentleman for the remainder of his days. Jennison had different notions: you might, perhaps, pass as a gentleman on a pound a day, but a pound a day was not everything, and to be practical, ten shillings was precisely half, and there was neither excitement nor fun in being half a gentleman. But it was not gentility that Jennison craved for, and it was not money.

Three pound ten a week enabled him to live quite comfortably, but it was that easy, uneventful, smooth-running comfort that something in him objected to. He wanted adventure; any sort of adventure. Nothing ever happened to him, either at the warehouse or at the lodgings; he was one of several at the first, and a veritable hermit at the second. With him one day was as another day, and Sundays and Bank Holidays were worse than the rest. Sometimes, of course, he got a little excited over his wooings of the Muse; now and then his heart jumped when he got an oblong envelope from some magazine editor or other, and, for a few seconds, allowed himself to wonder whether it contained a proof or an oft-rejected manuscript.

And sometimes he dared to let himself think of giving the firm a month's notice, drawing his small store of saved money out of the Post Office Savings Bank, and going boldly, rashly, adventurously, into a world of which he dreamed much and knew next to nothing. But though Jennison had been four years in London, his brains were still essentially rustic, and they cooled at the motive when he fairly faced it; after all, seventy silver shillings, paid regularly every Friday afternoon, is something that you mustn't sneeze at...besides, there was the annual rise. No! He was tied to the warehouse, and the grip of the knot didn't hurt...still, he longed for adventure, wished that things would happen...something...anything... If Jennison had only known it, something was just about to happen in Cartwright Gardens when he put his head out of his window and looked round. It was a clear night...for London and the moon was at the full.

Cartwright Gardens was quiet and deserted: a light shone here and there in a window, but there was not a soul to be seen on either pavement or roadway. Suddenly a man came round the corner, out of Mabledon Place. The moon shone directly upon him; Jennison saw all of him distinctly. He was a tallish, well-built man, agile of movement; he walked well and smartly; Jennison thought he was in a hurry. He carried a walking-stick, and as he came along he was swinging it jauntily. But all of a sudden, when he was some ten or twelve yards away from the house out of which Jennison watched him, he cast the stick away from him, let out a strange, half-stifled cry, and, lifting both hands, began tearing at his neck-wear, as if he was being throttled.

For a second or two his actions were frantic; then, still more suddenly, his uplifted hands dropped at his sides, his figure swayed this way and that, and with a scarcely-perceptible moan he plunged straight forward on the pavement and rolled over into the gutter. And there he lay as still as the stonework beneath him and Jennison made a dive for his door and rushed headlong to the street.

All the folk who lived in No. 85 had gone to bed by that time, and the landlady, knowing that there was no late-comer to arrive, had locked and bolted her front door. It took Jennison a minute or two to turn the key and draw the two bolts, and all the time something was pulsing and throbbing in his brain, and saying over and over and over again. You'll find the man dead! You'll find the man dead! And when at last he had got clear of the house, and had rushed along the street to where the man lay, quiet enough, in the gutter, and had bent down and laid a hand on him, he knew that the man was dead...dead, Jennison informed himself, in non-original fashion, as a door-nail.

Jennison was puzzled. He knew that a man can be all alive one minute and all dead the next. He had read...being inquisitive about such things...many newspaper reports of executions, and had gloated morbidly over the fact that from the moment of quitting the condemned cell to that in which death took place on the adjacent scaffold only thirty-five seconds had elapsed; he understood, too, that in electrocutions, the actual passage from life to death was even quicker...far quicker. But those things weren't close at hand...this had been. Three, or at most, five minutes previously he had seen this man marching jauntily, bravely along, swinging his stick...now he lay there at Jennison's feet as dead as...again he caught at a hackneyed phrase...as dead as Queen Anne. And Queen Anne, reflected Jennison, thinking queerly, had been dead...oh, no end of time! Dead! but she wasn't any deader than this chap!

There had been no noise, and so no windows went up in Cartwright Gardens. And just then no one came along, in either direction; Jennison was alone with the man who lay there so quietly. He bent down again and looked more closely at him. As far as he could judge, in the light of the street lamp and the glow of the moon, this was a man of about thirty-five years of age, a good-looking, even handsome man, a man, evidently, of some position and means, for he was well-dressed in a smartly-cut suit of dark blue serge, and had good linen, and a gold watch chain across his vest. His hat had fallen from him when he fell, and lay a yard or two away. Jennison picked it up and looked abstractedly into the lining. There, without feeling that he saw, he read the name and address of a Liverpool hatter, and turning the hat about in his hands noticed that it was quite new...perhaps its wearer had just come from Liverpool? But anyway, there he lay, statuesquely still...dead.

"Must ha' been a fit!" mused Jennison, unable to run to great heights of speculation or theory. "A fit!...sudden. People do fall down and die in fits...die quick, too. So I've heard. It couldn't be anything but a fit. And what am I to do next?"

As if in immediate answer to this question, the sound of a heavy, regular step came to Jennison's ears. He knew that sound...a policeman was coming; he was coming into Cartwright Gardens from Marchmont Street. He came every midnight, almost to the minute, as Jennison, who often sat up late, tediously wooing the Muse, knew well.

Presently he appeared, and Jennison hurried to meet him, and arrived at the point of contact breathless. The policeman halted, staring, but impassive.

"Oh, I say!" began Jennison lamely. "I...the fact is, there's a dead man lying up there, nearly opposite our house. I...I think I saw him die. From my window, you know."

The policeman quickened. He might have been a warhorse, sniffing the battle, or a fox-hound, catching a whiff of scent. His eyes opened wider, and he looked along the pavement, following Jennison's ink-stained forefinger.

"Oh!" he exclaimed. "Just so! And..."

At that moment he caught sight of the dark heap lying in the gutter, and he relapsed into official silence and strode off, Jennison ambling at his side.

"Yes!" said Jennison jerkily. "I...I saw him! I was looking out of the window...my window...No. 85 I live...third floor. He came along, walking quickly, swinging his stick...I've an idea he was whistling or humming a tune. Then...suddenly stopped! Tore at his throat...extraordinary motions! And then he fell! and rolled into the gutter. And when I got down to him he was dead; oh, quite dead. What do you think it could have been?"

But all the policeman vouchsafed to say was in the form of a question, put staccato fashion.

"When was this?"

"Just now, two or three minutes since," replied Jennison. He heaved a deep sigh...a sigh of speculative surprise. "Lord!" he muttered. "It doesn't seem...it isn't...more than five or six minutes when I first saw him!"

"Doesn't take long to die?" observed the policeman sententiously. "Thing is...here or elsewhere, I reckon! cause of death." Then having a bright notion, he added, "P'raps you're mistaken, may be unconscious?"

But they were close to the fallen man now, and the policeman, after a hasty examination, looked up at Jennison and nodded.

"You're right," he said. "Dead enough! And...nobody with him, eh? No attack on him?"

"Attack?" exclaimed Jennison wonderingly. "Of course not! There wasn't a soul about."

The policeman began to fumble for his whistle.

"Then it must ha' been a fit," he said. "And there's fits ...and... fits! However..." He raised his whistle to his lips and blew. The silence seemed greater than ever when the sound had died away. Jennison stood, still staring at the inanimate thing in the gutter: the policeman fidgeted, shifting his weight from one foot to another. Suddenly he spoke, nodding at the dead man.

"You don't know him?"

Jennison started and looked up sharply.

"I?" he exclaimed. "Good Lord, no! Don't know him from...anybody!"

"What I meant was," said the policeman slowly, "what I meant was...you saying as how you lived...where? No. 85? and it being latish, and him here, I thought maybe you'd know him, say, by sight...dweller hereabouts, eh?"

"Never seen him in my life before!" declared Jennison. Then he caught sight of the dead man's hat, which he had carefully placed aside. "That hat," he continued, pointing to it. "I picked it up. Liverpool, it says in it—maker's or seller's name, you know. P'raps he's a Liverpool man. You'd think so, wouldn't you? Liverpool being in the hat?"

"Oh, well, his clothing'll be examined," remarked the policeman easily. "There'll be something on him, likely or not. Papers...cards...such like. He'll be taken to the mortuary—as soon as we can get the ambulance. Doctor'll have to see him, too. Then...."

He broke off as men came round the near corners. Jennison wondered that so many came so quickly. One...two...three...four...five policemen; a sergeant among them. He had to tell his tale to the sergeant; he told it in detail while others went for an ambulance. And when that came the sergeant asked Jennison to go with them: the police station and the mortuary, he said, were close together, and Jennison, as the only eye-witness, had better tell his story to the inspector. Jennison was nothing loath; here, at last, was an adventure, a mystery.

But it had drab, dismal settings, he thought, presently. The mortuary was a cold, repellent place, and it looked all the colder and more repellent, somehow, when they had laid the dead man there. A police surgeon came and examined what they had fetched him to see: he was one of those men, thought Jennison, out of whom you're not going to extract speech if they don't want to speak; he did his job in a silence which none of those standing by cared or dared to break. But when he had done it he turned, looking round.

"Where's the man who saw him fall?" he asked sharply.

Jennison, who had remained hidden by the big forms around him, was shoved forward; the police surgeon sized him up in a quick glance.

"Well?" he said.

Jennison had to tell the tale again; this was the third time. The medical man listened in as grim a silence as he had kept before. But again his lips opened.

"Lifted his hands to his throat, you say?" he asked. "Suddenly?"

"All of a sudden!" answered Jennison. "One second he was walking along, ordinarily, the next, up went his hands, clutching, snatching, tearing at his throat! Like this...only worse!"

"Scream? Cry out?" asked the doctor.

"No...o" said Jennison. "Not what you'd call by either name. Made a bit of a moan...in his throat...as he went down."

"Face first?"

"Face first it was...fell right on his face, I think. Then," concluded Jennison, "then...well, he just rolled over into the gutter! And...lay still."

He looked round as he said the last word, and became aware that two other men had come into the room and were listening intently. One was a tall, soldierly-looking man in an inspector's uniform; the other was a quiet-looking, but sharp-eyed young man in civilian clothes. The surgeon turned to them, too, and after some muttered conversation about an inquest, went away. Jennison gathered that there would be a lot more to be heard about this affair...a lot more! And then, as nobody told him to go, or, indeed, took any particular notice of him, he stood by while the quiet-looking young man, whom presently he discovered to be a detective, and who answered to the name of Womersley, examined the dead man's clothing, going through pocket after pocket, and laying out the various contents. There was nothing very remarkable. Money was there, in some quantity; a good watch and chain; a pocket-book, in which were clippings from American papers, all relating to trade matters, a cigar case; a silver matchbox; a pocket-knife. But there were no letters, nothing to give any clue to the man's identity, until Womersley drew from a waistcoat pocket a crumpled visiting card with which, after a glance at it, he turned to the inspector.

"That's the only thing there is that's any use to us—now," he said.

"See? Thomas Bradmore, 157A Hunter Street. Is it...his? Or has it been given to him?"

"Close by, anyway," remarked the inspector. "Better go round there at once."

The detective moved off towards the door, without further words. And Jennison quietly slipped after him. It was his adventure and he was going on with it.

Chapter 2

Nobody offered any objection to Jennison's departure. He had already given his name and address to the sergeant, and since his last statement to the police surgeon, nobody had taken any notice of him. He felt, somehow, that he was unimportant, a very minor pawn in the game: he slunk, rather than marched, out of the door and the building. All the same, once outside, he made up to the detective.

"May I go with you?" he asked, half afraid of his temerity. "I...I'd like to, if you don't mind."

Womersley, who seemed somewhat abstracted, half paused and stared at his interrogator...wonderingly. In the light of the neighboring lamp, he sized up Jennison and smiled.

"Oh!" he said. "You're the chap that saw, aren't you? Just so!"

"I saw!" assented Jennison. "Everything!"

"Why do you want to go with me?" demanded Womersley. "Eh?"

"Because I did see," answered Jennison. "Now I want to hear."

Womersley laughed. The laugh was half satirical, but the other half was wholly indulgent, and he nodded his head and turned along the pavement.

"Well, I don't know why you shouldn't," he said. "And, as it happens, I'm not quite sure where this Hunter Street is. I'm new to this quarter of the town...I only came here, on special business, yesterday. Now up crops this!"

"I know where Hunter Street is," remarked Jennison, eager to be of use. "Two minutes' walk...as a matter of fact, it's close to Cartwright Gardens. I'll take you straight there." Then, when they had crossed the road and walked on a little, he said timidly, "I suppose you're a detective, aren't you?"

"That's it!" answered Womersley. "Detective-Sergeant, Criminal Investigation Department, Scotland Yard—...ow you've got it!"

"It must be very interesting work," suggested Jennison.

"Sometimes!" said Womersley, with another laugh. "And sometimes...t'other thing. Dull!"

"I should have thought it could never have been that!" remarked Jennison.

"Dare say!" replied Womersley. "Fact, though! Horribly dull...at times. Prosaic!"

Jennison ruminated over this. He had a conception of detectives...formed entirely from his own imagination; he also had an idea of what a detective ought to look like. And Womersley wasn't a bit like it...he was quite an ordinary young man in appearance; Jennison saw thousands and thousands of his type every day in the City. But there being no doubt that Womersley was a genuine detective, he proceeded to cultivate him.

"What now," asked Jennison, in the accents of a disciple who finds himself admitted to the presence of a known master, "what, now, would you say is the particular gift or faculty that a detective ought to possess?"

Womersley laughed again. Then he threw two words over his shoulder. "Common sense!" he said.

"Nothing beyond?" asked Jennison, in surprise.

"If you like," laughed Womersley, "still more common sense...and still more common sense after that. I'm not defining common sense, you know. But...common sense all the time! that's the ticket. This Hunter Street? Well, the number's 157A."

The house was close by, and it was all in darkness. But there was a bell and a knocker at the front door, and repeated recourse to each prefaced the throwing up of a window-sash on the second floor and the protrusion of a head. A man's voice sounded above them.

"What is it?—who's there?"

"Is this Mr. Bradmore's?" inquired Womersley. "Mr. Thomas Bradmore?"

"I'm Mr. Bradmore," replied the man. "What do you want?"

Womersley glanced up and down the deserted street.

Then he looked up.

"Sorry to rouse you, Mr. Bradmore," he answered. "A man died very suddenly in Cartwright Gardens about an hour ago. We found your card on him. Can you come down and tell me if you know anything of him?"

The voice spoke one word.

"Wait!"

The window snapped with a click, and Womersley turned to Jennison.

"That settles that," he murmured. "The dead man isn't Bradmore. Next thing is...does Bradmore know who he is?"

Before Jennison had had time to speculate on the chances for and against this, the door opened, and Bradmore himself appeared, clad in an old dressing-gown and holding a lamp above his head. He was a tall, middle-aged man, somewhat worn and melancholy of aspect, whose dark, straggling hair and beard were already shot with gray, and who looked, somehow, as if he had known trouble and anxiety. He made a steady inspection of both men before speaking; Jennison he passed over quickly; at Womersley he looked longer.

"Police?" he asked.

"Scotland Yard man, Mr. Bradmore," replied Womersley. He drew out the crumpled card which he had found on the dead man, and thrust it into the rays of the lamp. "That's the card I spoke of, Mr. Bradmore. Yours, isn't it?"

Bradmore nodded, and motioned his visitors to enter. He closed the door after them, and, leading them into a room on the right hand side of the passage, set his lamp on a center table, pointed the two men to chairs, and himself took one facing the detective. And he immediately put a direct question to Womersley.

"What like was this man?"

"Good-looking, fresh-colored man, Mr. Bradmore," replied Womersley, promptly. "About thirty-five years old, I should say. Well dressed...dark blue serge suit. Plenty of money in his pockets. But no papers...at least, none giving any name or address, except, of course, your card. That was in the right-hand waistcoat pocket."

"And you say he died suddenly in Cartwright Gardens?" asked Bradmore. "Of...what?"

Womersley shook his head and pointed to Jennison, who was listening with all his ears.

"That's a question for the doctor, Mr. Bradmore," he answered. "This young man saw all there was to be seen. He saw the man come along the street, apparently in the best of health and spirits, suddenly throw up his hands and clutch at his throat, and then fall to the ground and die...at once!"

Bradmore gave Jennison a glance. But it was no more than a glance. His attention went back to the detective.

"What exact time was this?" he asked.

"According to our friend here," answered Womersley, again indicating Jennison, "just about a quarter to twelve. But...do you know who the man is, Mr. Bradmore? That's the important thing just now."

Bradmore nodded, slowly.

"Yes!" he answered. "It'll be Alfred Jakyn...Alfred Jakyn!"

"Yes?" said Womersley. "And...who is Alfred Jakyn? Was, of course, I should say. Who was he, exactly?"

Bradmore began to stroke his beard, looking reflectively at his questioner.

"Do you know Holborn...I mean, do you know it well?" he asked.

"No," replied Womersley, "I don't; my work, as a rule, is at the other end of the town."

"I thought not," said Bradmore, "or you'd have known the name of Jakyn. If you go along Holborn tomorrow morning, you'll see, at the corner of Counsel's Passage, a chemist's shop...well known...with the name Daniel Jakyn over it. As a matter of fact, Daniel Jakyn's dead, and I'm his successor: I took over the business, of which I'd been manager for several years, when he died, last spring. And Alfred Jakyn was his son...only son. Only child, in fact."

"Just so," said Womersley. "And what do you know about Alfred, Mr. Bradmore? I mean, of course, in relation to his sudden death?"

"I can soon tell you all I know about Alfred Jakyn," replied Bradmore. "As I've said, he was his father's only child. As a boy and a young man, he was a wild and extravagant fellow...he gave his father a lot of trouble, and caused him no end of expense. About ten years ago he disappeared, and, as far as I know...in fact, I'm certain about it...his father never heard a word of him from that time until the time of his own death. I never knew of any one who ever heard of him; I certainly never did...until yesterday evening. Then...about a quarter to eight he walked into my shop..."

"You're speaking of last evening...present night, as you may call it?" interrupted Womersley. "Same night as that in which he died?"

"Just so," assented Bradmore. "Last evening...the evening that's just over. He came in, greeted me as if he'd seen me only the day before, told me he'd landed at Liverpool yesterday morning, from America...New York, I think and asked for news of his father. He didn't know, until I told him, that his father was dead. Hearing that, he sat down in the parlor at the back of the shop to hear all I had to tell him."

"You'd no doubt have a good deal to tell, Mr. Bradmore?" suggested Womersley.

"Well, yes!" replied Bradmore. "He seemed to know nothing. He looked prosperous, as far as you could judge from outward appearances, but I couldn't make out where he'd been most of the time during the ten years absence, for in addition to not knowing anything about his father, he seemed to be remarkably ignorant about things in general...I mean things that have happened of late years."

"Um!" murmured Womersley. "Maybe he's been where news doesn't run. However..."

"I told him all there was to tell about his family affairs," continued Bradmore. "I told him, to begin with, that his father died intestate...left no will at all..."

"Much to leave?" asked Womersley.

"Yes, a great deal...he was a well-to-do man," replied Bradmore. "Of course, as Alfred had turned up, it would all come to him. He recognized that. But I also told him that his relations were already taking action to have his death presumed, as he hadn't been heard of for ten years, so that they could succeed to Daniel's property..."

"There are relations, then?" interrupted Womersley.

"Yes. Daniel Jakyn had a sister-in-law, Mrs. Nicolas Jakyn, widow of his younger brother. She has two children, a son, Nicholas, and a daughter, with the odd name of Belyna. Mrs. Nicholas Jakyn and her children...they're both grown up...live with Mrs. Nicholas's brother, Dr. Cornelius Syphax, in Brunswick Square, close by here. If Alfred Jakyn had died during his absence abroad, the Nicholas Jakyn family, of course, came in for Daniel's money. And they're now...believing Alfred to be dead, abroad...in process of trying to get it. I took over the business under arrangement with them...sanctioned by the Courts, of course."

"You told him all this, last evening?" asked Womersley.

"Of course. He laughed at it, and said that as he was very much alive, all that would come to an end. And," continued Bradmore, "after talking things over a little more with me, he went away to call at Brunswick Square, to let Mrs. Nicholas Jakyn and her children know that he was living and had come home again. That was the last I saw of him."

"Just so," said Womersley. "Um! well, a few questions, Mr. Bradmore. To start with...what time did he leave the shop in Holborn?"

"Just about half-past eight."

"To go straight to Brunswick Square?"

"So I understood."

"Why did you give him your card...the card with your private address on it?"

"Because he said that he'd likely want to see me after he'd seen his aunt and his cousins, and as I was going home I told him where I lived...gave him the card you've brought here just now."

"I see! Did he tell you where he was staying in London?"

"He did. At the Euston Hotel."

"Did he ask you anything else, Mr. Bradmore? anything that we ought to know? Because, I may as well tell you that the police-surgeon who made a preliminary examination of the body is highly suspicious...he thinks there's been foul play...and, naturally, we want to know all we can. Did Alfred Jakyn ask you about any people he'd known in the old days? Did he give you any idea that there was anybody he wanted to see again, or wanted to find?"

"Oh, well," answered Bradmore, after reflecting a moment, "there was just one question he asked me, as he was leaving. That was if I knew anything of the whereabouts of a young woman named Millie Clover, who at one time had been employed at the shop in Holborn as a clerk. I didn't...hadn't heard of her for years."

"Nothing else?"

"Nothing!" answered Bradmore, with decision. "I've told you everything."

Womersley nodded, rose, and began to button his overcoat.

"Queer business, isn't it?" he said, in matter-of-fact tones. "You say he seemed to be in first-class condition...as regards health?"

"I should say he was certainly in the very best of health and spirits," assented Bradmore. "Alert, vigorous, cheerful...all that. Oh, yes!"

"And then he goes and dies in the most mysterious fashion, all in a minute!" said Womersley. "Well, as it is, they'll want you at the inquest, you know, Mr. Bradmore...you'll be hearing about it, in due course."

"I imagine that we shall all hear a great deal about a good many things, in due course," remarked Bradmore, as he led his visitors to the door. "I know what I think, from what you've told me!"

"And that's...what?" asked Womersley.

"No, no! I'll keep that to myself!" said Bradmore. "Maybe the coroner's jury will eventually be led to the same conclusion...we shall see!"

He closed the door on them, and Womersley and Jennison turned again into the night. The detective produced and lighted a pipe.

"Well, that's a beginning!" he said as they moved away. "Easy start, too!"

"What shall you do...now?" asked Jennison, eagerly. "What next?"

"Drop in at the police station for a minute or two, and then...bed!" answered Womersley. "Just that!"

"You can sleep...after this sort of thing?" exclaimed Jennison.

"Try me!" said Womersley. "Oh, yes, I can sleep! Well...good-night."

Their ways parted there, and Jennison moved forward slowly, through Compton Street to Cartwright Gardens. Very soon he came to the spot, close to his own house, whereat the mysterious Alfred Jakyn had fallen and died. He stood staring at it, wondering, speculating; thinking how queer it all was. Suddenly he saw something that lay in the gutter, near the place from which the policemen had lifted the dead man's body, something that gleamed white in the moonlight. Stooping and picking it up, he found it to be a scrap of paper, tightly twisted into what one called a cocked-hat. There was writing inside—plain enough that, when he had untwisted it. But Jennison's eyesight was not over good, and in that light he could make nothing of what he saw to be there. And at that he let himself into the house and hurried up to his own room. The light still burned above the mantelpiece, and he got beneath it, smoothed out the crumpled bit of paper, and read what was written on it. The handwriting was a woman's...pretty, well-formed writing, even if it looked hurried. And the words were just nine in number: West corner of Endsleigh Gardens in half an hour.

Chapter 3

Adventures were crowding thick and fast on Jennison, but this scrap of paper business was more to his taste than any that had preceded it during that eventful midnight. This, he said to himself, was a bit of all right; it was the sort of thing you read of in newspapers and novels. He read and re-read the nine words, reveling in their mysteriousness, gloating over the fact that it was he, and he only, who had found this paper on which they were written. Suddenly a terrible suspicion over-clouded the brightness of his ideas...how did he know that this bit of writing had anything to do with the dead man? It might have been dropped into the gutter from whence he had rescued it by somebody else; it might have nothing whatever to do with Alfred Jakyn and his strange death.

But considering everything, Jennison believed that it had...he cast his doubt aside. No!—the note had probably been thrust by Alfred Jakyn loosely, carelessly, into the edge of a pocket, and had fallen out on the street when he fell. And it might prove a thing of high importance...what, he believed, the detectives call a clue. He began to wonder what Womersley would say when he showed it to him. But at that point temptation assailed Jennison. Why should he tell Womersley anything about this discovery? Why should not he, Albert Jennison, take a hand himself in the solving of the mystery? Why not? Why not, indeed? He went to bed on that, and turned and turned half the night, inventing theories and planning campaigns.

And when he woke in the morning, Jennison wished that he had nothing to do but to follow up this affair. He would have liked to go round to the police station to find Womersley and persuade that phlegmatic person to let him share in his investigations; perhaps, if Womersley had proved tractable, he might have let him into his own secret and shown him the scrap of paper. But he was a slave! a miserable, treadmill slave and nine o'clock found him, as usual, in the city. There he toiled all day, doing his work badly, for once, because his mind was otherwise. A thrill ran through him, however, when, as he entered his lodgings that evening, his landlady came up from her region in the basement bearing an official-looking piece of paper.

"There's been a policeman here after you, Mr. Jennison," she said, eyeing him closely. "He said to give you this here as soon as you come in."

Jennison glanced at the document and held his head a couple of inches higher.

"Ah, yes, Mrs. Canby," he answered. "Yes! It's about an inquest tomorrow morning. I'm a witness, you know...the most important witness, I believe. That poor fellow who died outside here last night, you know...I told you about it before I went out, you know."

"You did, Mr. Jennison, and a turn it did give me, too!" said Mrs. Canby. "To think of a feller-being falling dead outside there, and us all a-warm and snug in our beds, close by! Leastways, you weren't, Mr. Jennison. And how will it turn, Mr. Jennison, do you think?"

But Jennison didn't know. His only answer as he repaired to his tea-supper was to shake his head with dark and solemn meaning. What he did know, and highly appreciated, was that he was going to have a whole holiday next day. The inquest was set down for ten-thirty in the morning; of course he would have to be there, and probably the proceedings would last over several hours; anyway, being, as it were, specially commanded by the law to be present, he would certainly not be able to attend to his usual duties.

It gave him a thoroughly exquisite pleasure to write a letter to the manager of the warehouse explaining why he should not be at his desk next day, and for the rest of the evening, instead of writing poetry, he rehearsed his evidence, and even studied, before his mirror, the pose and attitude he would adopt in the witness-box. Next morning he spent much time over his toilet, and when he finally reached the Coroner's Court, a quarter of an hour earlier than he need have done, he was disgusted to find that all the other people assembled there seemed to have arrayed themselves in their oldest instead of their newest clothes: the prevailing tone of things was shabby, sordid. Jennison had never been in a coroner's court before. He was not impressed. The Coroner, a barrister, seemed to him too matter of fact and practical in his remarks; the jury, twelve good men and true, looked as if brains were much wanting among them; the police, the legal folk, the pressmen, the spectators, were all common, vulgar, material...there was too much of a business about it altogether, and none of that reserve and mystery which Jennison had hoped for. And at first the proceedings were very dull, because Jennison already knew all that came out. He had heard everything that Bradmore could tell, for instance. Bradmore, who gave formal proof of the dead man's identity, now re-told it; Jennison knew every word that was to come from him. And somehow, when he himself got into the witness-box, his performance there seemed dull and flat, and things weren't what he'd hoped they'd be. He had wanted to thrill the court with a thoroughly dramatic story; instead of that he found himself giving affirmatives and negatives to cut-and-dried questions.

There were no thrills; no sensations; actually some of the reporters present whispered and laughed among themselves while he, Jennison, the only man who had actually seen, was being examined. It was all as lifeless and sterile as the voice of the man who thrust a Testament into the hand of a witness and bade him or her repeat a babble of phrases. But Jennison, once more relegated to inconspicuousness among the herd of spectators, became conscious that the court was waking up when the police surgeon went into the witness-box. He had closely watched this functionary on the night of Alfred Jakyn's death, and had said to himself since that he knew as much about it as he, Jennison, did.

What Jennison did not know, however, was that since that hasty examination at the mortuary there had been an autopsy. But the Coroner knew, and the jury knew, and the legal folk present knew; so did the reporters, who, on the medical man's appearance, took seriously to their pencils and note-books. And in a couple of minutes Jennison found himself gasping at a suddenly-sprung suggestion. It hit him full, as the result of a brief question from the coroner and a sharp reply from the witness. They had already exchanged a good deal in the way of question and answer before this came along, but when it came, the atmosphere changed from heaviness to the quick instinct of surprise.

"And the result of the post-mortem examination, now? Have you formed any opinion as to the cause of death?"

"Yes. I am firmly of opinion as to the cause of death. Poison!"

The Coroner glanced at his jury. But each juryman was attentive enough; the twelve pairs of eyes were fixed steadily on the police surgeon.

"Poison!" repeated the Coroner. "What particular poison?"

"That I cannot say. It is a question for experts. We have already called in their aid. But I am convinced that the man was poisoned."

"From what you saw, you don't feel justified in particularizing?"

"I may say this. I believe the man was poisoned by something with the nature of which I and I should say, most medical practitioners...am unfamiliar. Judging from the evidence of the witness, Jennison, I think that the poison was administered to the deceased some time...probably two or three hours...previous to his death, and that the effect came with startling suddenness."

"Causing instantaneous death?"

"I think so."

The Coroner hesitated a moment, again glancing at the jury as if he wondered whether any juryman wanted to ask a question. But the jurymen were all staring silently and speculatively at the witness, and to him the Coroner turned once more. "When will the experts you mentioned be able to report?"

"Possibly in about a week or ten days."

"We can adjourn for a week, and then again, if necessary," said the Coroner. "But, there is another witness...oh, two witnesses, eh? that we had better hear this morning..." he bent from his desk to speak to the chief police official. "Oh, just so!" he added. "A relation of the dead man, eh?...just so."

The police surgeon stepped down from the witness box; the man who stood by it lifted a loud voice, staring into the crowd.

"Belyna Jakyn!"

Until that moment Jennison had paid little attention to the people around him: he had been too full of himself, too much preoccupied of his own part in this act of the drama. But now, hearing some slight commotion and murmuring among the crowded room behind him, he turned and looked in the direction to which the Coroner's officer had directed his summons. And there he saw four people, sitting together, and was quick-witted enough to set them down at once as the relations of Alfred Jakyn of whom Bradmore had spoken to Womersley and himself.

There was a tall, elderly man with a clever, clean-shaven face, a mass of dark hair, turning gray, an aquiline, aggressive nose, and a pair of peculiarly bright and burning black eyes; him he took to be Dr. Syphax, of Brunswick Square. Next him, and closely resembling him, and, if possible, of an even more intent cast of countenance and expression, was a woman who affected an old-fashioned style of dress, and was accordingly conspicuous among those about her; this, thought Jennison, must be Mrs. Nicholas Jakyn, aunt-in-law of the dead man. At her side sat a young man, smartly dressed, very ordinary of looks, who was assiduously sucking the knob of his walking-stick and scowling at the things in front, as if he considered the whole affair a rotten bore: he, doubtless, was Mrs. Nicholas Jakyn's son. And next to him was a young woman, who, as Jennison looked, was rising from her seat in response to the call, and who, of course, was the person called...Belyna Jakyn.

Everybody in court was staring at Belyna Jakyn. There was reason. Nature had been anything but kind to her. She was deformed: it was evident that she had been deformed from birth. She was a hunchback; one leg, it was obvious, was shorter than its fellow; she walked with some difficulty. But she was calm and self-possessed, and the face which she turned full on Coroner and jury was distinguished by good features, superior intelligence, and alert eyes; misshapen as the body was, any observant person could see that Belyna Jakyn had excellent brains. And she showed no sign of nervousness as she waited to be questioned; eyes and lips were calm and composed; the thin, white hands which rested on the ledge of the box were wholly at rest: the crowd of people, seeing all this, became as quiet as this new figure in the drama, listening intently. Belyna Jakyn, daughter of Mrs. Nicholas Jakyn, and niece of Daniel Jakyn, deceased, and therefore cousin of Alfred Jakyn, into the cause of whose death the Court was inquiring...to all this the witness assented, quietly. The Coroner, nodding his head at each answer, bent more confidentially towards the witness-box as he launched into more pertinent questions.

"I understand that you, and your mother, and your brother, live with your uncle...maternal uncle, I think...Dr. Cornelius Syphax, in Brunswick Square, Miss Jakyn?"

"We do!"

"Did Alfred Jakyn come to Dr. Syphax's house on Monday evening?"

"He did."

"Were you all at home?"

"No. There was no one at home but myself."

"You received him?"

"Yes."

"Did you recognize him as your cousin Alfred?"

"Oh, yes! I remembered him quite well. It is eleven years since he went away...ten or eleven, at any rate...but I was then twelve years old. Yes, I knew him at once."

"He entered the house?"

"He came first to the surgery, at the side of the house. I was there alone, making up medicines; I act as dispenser to Dr. Syphax. As soon as I saw who it was, I took him into the house, to the dining-room. We sat down there, to talk."

"Yes...and what did you talk about?"

"He did most of the talking. He told me he had been knocking about all over the world, and had been in some strange places and seen many strange things. He appeared to have heard very little of English, of even of European, affairs, of late years. He said that he had only landed in England, at Liverpool, early that morning, and did not know that his father was dead until he called on Mr. Bradmore on reaching London, in the evening. Then he said that Mr. Bradmore had told him that my uncle...his father...had left no will, and that, of course, everything would come to him, and he added that he would see that my mother, my brother, and myself were not forgotten."

"He was very friendly then?"

"Very! He seemed in good spirits...high spirits. He joked

and laughed about things, and said he would call again next day at a time when we should all be at home, and that then we would go into family matters."

"Did he tell you anything that made you think he had prospered during his absence?"

"Not particularly. He did say, half jokingly, that he hadn't come back empty-handed."

"Did he say whether he had married during his absence?"

"No...he told me nothing of that sort, nothing about his private concerns, beyond what I have told you. He was not with me very long."

"That's what I'm coming to, Miss Jakyn. Now, what time was it when he came to your surgery?"

"About a quarter to nine o'clock."

"And he left the house...when?"

"About ten minutes past nine."

"Did he give you any address in London?"

"Yes...he said he was staying at the Euston Hotel...simply because it was at hand when he got out of the train, he added, with a laugh. He said he should stay there for a week or two, now he'd got there."

"Did he mention any appointment for that evening ing to meet anybody?"

"No. He only said he'd come back and stay longer next day."

This was all that was asked of Belyna Jakyn; she was followed in the witness box by a young man who described himself as a waiter at the Euston Hotel, and testified that, having seen the body of Alfred Jakyn, he recognized it as that of a gentleman who was in and about the hotel on Monday evening last. He had seen him in the dining-room from 6.30 to 7 o'clock that evening: he saw him again in the smoking-room later in the evening.

"Can you be sure of the exact time on the last occasion?" asked the Coroner.

"Yes, sir," replied the witness. "The gentleman came into the smoking-room about half-past nine; I got him a whiskey and soda. He sat down for a while. There was nobody much about just then, and while he was there, I noticed him particularly."

"For what reason?"

"Well, sir, he seemed restless. He fidgeted, first in one place, then another. He walked about the room, muttering. In the end, a bit before ten o'clock, he pulled a bit of paper out of his waistcoat pocket, and seemed to read something on it."

"Yes...and what then?"

"Then he suddenly turned on his heel, sir, and went very quickly away. That was the last I saw of him."

Chapter 4

At this stage of the proceedings the Coroner adjourned his inquiry for a week, warning his jurymen that when they once again assembled there might be another immediate adjournment, and that in any case they were to keep their minds open and not to pay too much attention to what they read in the newspapers about the affair which they were investigating.

Then the spectators began to go away, most of them grumbling that there had not been more of it, and Jennison drifted out with them, convinced that the scrap of paper now in his possession was identical with that of which the waiter from the Euston Hotel had just spoken. He was still undecided as to whether he would tell Womersley about that or whether he wouldn't. He looked round for Womersley; the detective, near the outer door of the court, was giving audience to the pressmen who were putting eager questions to him; Jennison sidled close up to the group, and nobody reproving him for his intrusion, he stayed there and listened.

"I may as well tell you fellows all that it's necessary you should put in your papers...at present," Womersley was saying. "Save you asking me a lot of questions, anyway! Just this, then...this man, Alfred Jakyn, came to the Euston Hotel on Monday afternoon, late, and booked a room there. He dined in the hotel, and went out...you've heard about his movements during the evening. We know where he was between, say, eight o'clock and ten o'clock. First, he was with Bradmore, in Holborn. Then he was with Miss Belyna Jakyn at Brunswick Square. Then he was for half an hour or so in the smoking-room at the Euston Hotel. The problem is...where was he between ten o'clock, when he once more left the hotel, and a quarter to twelve, when the witness Jennison...who's standing behind you...saw him fall dead in Cartwright Gardens? Did he go to meet any one? If so, whom? If he was poisoned and the doctors are sure he was!...who poisoned him? Did he poison himself? That's not likely. If somebody else poisoned him, he was murdered. Why? There you are!...plenty of copy for you there!"

"Go on!" murmured one of the reporters. "There's more than that, Womersley. Of course you've examined his room and so on?"

"Yes, you can have that," assented the detective. "At his room in the hotel, two suit-cases, with plenty of good clothing, linen, and so on: the things that a well-to-do man would have. No papers of any importance...no private letters...nothing much in that way, except that in a wallet is a draft on the Equitable Trust Company of New York, at their London branch in King William Street, for ten thousand dollars. Nothing to show what his business was, nor any business addresses. But in one suit-case was a packet of recently-taken photographs...taken in New York and I'm going to hand over a couple of them to you fellows; you can manage about reproducing them as you please. Somebody, seeing them, may recognize the man, and be able to tell something about him. Here you are! and that's the lot."

The reporters seized on the photographs, and Womersley thrust his hands in his pockets and sauntered off. Jennison was after him.

"Do...do you happen to want me for anything?" he asked. "I..."

Womersley scarcely looked at him as he replied, flinging the words over his shoulder.

"Not that I know of, my friend!" he answered. "Done your bit in there, haven't you?"

He went on his way, and Jennison, feeling distinctly snubbed, shrank back, hurt and mortified. But he revived quickly when the youngest of the reporters, catching sight of him, and recognising him as the man who had actually seen Alfred Jakyn die, approached and began to question him. The reporter suggested an adjournment to the nearest saloon bar; there, under the influence of a glass of bitter ale or two, Jennison's tongue wagged freely. He gave his new friend a full and elaborate account of what he had seen, and exhibited what his listener generously called unusual histrionic ability in acting the part of the dying man. The reporter, youthful and ardent, and attached to a paper which catered for a horrors-loving public, welcomed Jennison as a distinct find. But even Jennison became exhausted at last in the sense that he could tell no more...to that audience, at any rate.

"Queer business," mused the reporter. "And likely to work up into a first-rate mystery. Poisoning, eh? We haven't had a really first-class bit of poisoning since...well, since I came on my job!"

"You think it will be poisoning?" asked Jennison.

"Should say so, old man, after what the police surgeon said," replied his companion. "Sort of chap, that, that wouldn't say anything that he didn't mean. My notion, of course, is that he and the other doctor he mentioned know already that the man was poisoned, but they want the verdict and backing of these big bugs...experts, you know...what do they call 'em...toxicologists. Lot of fine stuff to be got out of an A1 poison case, my boy! I know a chap who's a medical student...at Bart.'s he is...and he tells me that there are poisons that you can administer to a man, and that he'd know nothing about it for hours, never feel any ill effects, you know, and go about as chirpy and fit as you like, and then, all of a sudden...all over, my boy!—quick as having a bullet through your brain. Or...quicker!"

"That's what must have happened in this case," said Jennison. "But...who gave it to him?"

"Ah! that's the question!" exclaimed the reporter. "A question for the police. Well, the Press will do what it can. That is, as far as I'm concerned. Press and Police! a mighty combination! Well, so long, old man; going to write it up now."

He went away hurriedly, and Jennison, finding that the morning had worn to his usual dinner hour, repaired to a restaurant which he occasionally patronized, and on the strength of his holiday, did himself very well. And while he ate and drank, he thought. It began to strike him as a queer and significant thing that, granting the cause of Alfred Jakyn's death to be poison, nearly all the folks with whom it was known he had been in contact on the evening of his death were people who, from the very fact of their professions, must have poison at their disposal. There was Bradmore...Bradmore was a chemist...chemists have no end of poisons knocking about.

Then there was that Miss Belyna Jakyn, poor thing! Didn't she say in the witness-box that she was dispenser to her uncle, the doctor with the queer name? Of course, she'd have poisons in Dr. Syphax's surgery. Well, but why should Bradmore poison Alfred Jakyn? No motive at all for that...no! But as regards the young woman...ah! According to Bradmore, the Nicholas Jakyn family, just before the recent event, were taking steps to have Alfred Jakyn's death presumed, and to establish their claim to Daniel Jakyn's estate: the sudden arrival of Alfred, all alive and kicking, would upset their plans. Now supposing... supposing...supposing Miss Belyna, alone with cousin Alfred, and knowing that he stood between her and her family and a nice fortune, took the opportunity to give him a fatal dose of something...eh? It might be that Miss Belyna had made a special study of poisons, and was an expert in their use, or possible use. After all, said Jennison, you never can tell, you never know...

At this point a brilliant notion occurred to Jennison. How did he know, how did the Coroner know, how did the police know, that Miss Belyna Jakyn told the precise truth in the witness-box in which she had made such an odd, pathetic figure? She had said that nobody but herself saw Alfred Jakyn when he called at Brunswick Square. Was that true? Nobody, of course, could prove that it wasn't, for Alfred was dead. But perhaps Miss Belyna's evidence had been carefully cooked by the family? Jennison knew enough to know that as a rule doctors are in their surgeries of an evening...you were pretty safe to find them there, anyhow, between seven and nine.

Now supposing Alfred Jakyn got into the hands of Belyna Jakyn and her uncle, Dr. Syphax...eh? There was something very queer about Dr. Syphax, thought Jennison. His eyes were like lamps...and how he could stare! Odd man, very! and probably capable of poisoning anybody who stood in his way or interfered with his plans. And his sister, Mrs. Nicholas Jakyn, was a queer-looking woman. She reminded Jennison of a bird he had seen in a big cage at the Zoological Gardens...what was it? oh, a condor...yes, just that! Queer lot altogether, that Jakyn-Syphax combination...very. And Jennison, by this time warmed to his self-imposed task, began to wonder how he could get into the Brunswick Square house and see these people close at hand. Rubbing his forehead, which he usually called his brow. in deep thought over this, Jennison suddenly became aware of a fine excuse for calling on Dr. Syphax. For some little time past Jennison had been troubling himself about a small lump which was growing about an inch above his left eyebrow. He had thought little of it at first, when it was no bigger than a pea, but it had steadily increased in size, and was now as big as a cherry, and only the other day one of his fellow-clerks at the warehouse had said to him, lugubriously, that if he were Jennison, he'd have that seen to...he'd known a man, he said, who had a lump like that on his head, which, neglected and suffered to grow, became as big as an orange. Surgical advice, said this counselor, was what Jennison wanted, and sharp! And now, as he smoked a cigarette and sipped his black coffee...a drink that he loathed, but considered the correct thing to have when lunching at that particular restaurant...Jennison decided that his lump would furnish an excellent excuse for calling on Dr. Syphax. Forthwith he strolled round towards Brunswick Square, and very quickly discovered the doctor's dwelling. There was an alley at the side of the house, and a brass plate on the railing: there Jennison saw what he wanted...Surgery Hours, 9 a.m. To 10.30 a.m.: 6.30 p.m. To 9 p.m. Having ascertained that, he looked inquisitively at the house. Its windows were all heavily curtained, and it seemed to Jennison that it was essentially an abode of mystery.

At a quarter to seven that evening, Jennison, with a beating heart, tapped at the door of Dr. Syphax's surgery, opened it, walked in, and came face to face with the doctor, who, his tall, spare form clad in a white linen operating-jacket, was just about to let out a patient. He stared hard at the newcomer, and then suddenly smiled; it was the sort of smile, thought Jennison, that takes a devil of a lot of thinking about. There was a word for that sort of smile...what was it? Enigmatical! yes, that was it, enigmatical.

"Hallo!" exclaimed Dr. Syphax. "Seen you before today, young man! The witness of this morning, eh? Jennison?"

"Yes," assented Jennison. "That's why I called. At least, I mean...not because of that affair...nothing to do with that...but I heard you were a doctor, and living close by, and I want a doctor...never employed one before, though!"

"You're a lucky chap, then!" cried Dr. Syphax. "And

what's the matter?"

Jennison walked under the centre light of the surgery, and removing his cap pointed to the lump above his eyebrow.

"I want to know what that is?" he said, ingenuously. "That's what?"

"That's a cyst, my friend," answered Dr. Syphax promptly. "A cyst! that's what that is. And a cyst is a hollow growth filled with liquid secretion...sebaceous matter."

"Will it get bigger, if left alone?" asked Jennison.

"Rather," said Dr. Syphax heartily. "Big as...well, a walnut! Perhaps bigger. Might grow as big as the head it's on...if permitted."

"What's to be done to it, doctor?" asked Jennison.

"You must have it removed, of course," answered Syphax. "The sooner, the better. When I've removed it and extracted the root, then it'll be done with. Do it now if you like."

But Jennison thought not. He saw some scalpels and things lying around, and he didn't like the looks of them.

"I could come next Sunday morning," he suggested. "Would that do?"

"Quite well," assented Syphax. "Come at 10.30. Won't take long. Nor hurt you much either. A bit, of course."

"I'm in a city office," remarked Jennison. "Shall I have to take a few days off?"

"Oh, well..." said Syphax. "No particular need, but, of course, you'll have to wear bandages for a few days till the scar heals, you know."

Jennison silently decided that he would secure a week's holiday on the strength of that operation...perhaps a fortnight's. He picked up his cap.

"I'll come, Sunday morning, then," he said, awkwardly. "10.30. I thought
it would have to be done. A—a friend of mine said so. Good-night, doctor...I suppose you haven't heard any more about that matter we were engaged on this morning?"

"Nothing, my lad, nothing," answered Syphax. He was making an entry in a book that lay open on his desk, and he turned from it to glance at his patient with another queer smile. "Strange affair, eh?"

"It gave me a turn," said Jennison solemnly. "Of course,

I'd never seen anything like it! A man living...all alive, as you might say...one minute, and next as dead as...as..."

"As ever a man can be," suggested Syphax.

"Startling, to be sure...if you've never seen it," answered Jennison. "I heard that detective, Womersley, telling the reporters that he's searched the dead man's room at the Euston Hotel and hadn't found anything much there beyond a bank draft for ten thousand dollars. And some recently-taken photographs."

"Oh!" said Syphax. "Dear me! Well, I suppose there are a lot of things to be found out. Lots! Always are in these cases, you know, my friend."

"Do you think he was poisoned?" asked Jennison.

"Might have been! Why not? The police surgeon seemed to think so...to be sure of it, in fact," replied Syphax. "Of course, I can't say: I wasn't present at the autopsy. That'll come out." He hesitated a minute, watching Jennison good-humouredly. "I suppose you didn't see anybody following Alfred Jakyn, did you?" he asked suddenly. "Nobody looking round corners, or anything of that sort?"

Jennison jumped at the mere suggestion.

"I?" he exclaimed. "Good Lord, no, doctor! I'll take a solemn affidavit there wasn't a soul about! Neither up Cartwright Gardens nor down Cartwright Gardens. Why...why...do you think somebody was following him...watching him?"

Syphax was now busily engaged in compounding a bottle of medicine. Jennison watched his long, slim, white fingers moving among the drugs, and his lips mechanically whispering some formula. He repeated his question.

"Do you really, doctor?"

Syphax, filling up his bottle with distilled water, began to shake it violently. What was inside it gradually assumed a beautiful opalescent tint.

"Shouldn't wonder! shouldn't wonder at all!" he said at last. "No doubt you didn't see 'em, my lad...attention engaged other where...with...him. Very deep, black mystery indeed, Jennison—thousand feet deep! take a long time to touch bottom. Well...ten-thirty, Sunday morning."

Jennison felt himself dismissed and went out. At the top of the square he bought an evening newspaper; the paper of which the young reporter of that morning was representative. He swelled with pride and importance as his eyes encountered the columns of stuff about the Cartwright Gardens Affair, and saw his own name in capitals. And there was the interview with him and the reproduced photographs of Alfred Jakyn and lots more...

Jennison flew off to a favorite haunt of his. In a small side street off the Euston Road there was a quiet, highly respectable little tavern, the Cat and Bagpipe, whither he often repaired of an evening for a glass of ale and a chat with the barmaid, Chrissie Walker, a smart and lively young woman. He marched in now on Chrissie, and, finding her alone, laid the newspaper before her, pointing to his own name. But Chrissie's eyes went straight to the photograph of Alfred Jakyn, and she let out an exclamation that almost rose to a scream.

"Mercy on us!" she exclaimed, pointing to the reproduction. "Why, that man was in here on Monday night! he came in here with a lady!"

Chapter 5

During the last day or two Jennison had been slowly acquiring knowledge in the art and science of crime investigation, and had learned that one who desired to become a proficient should never show himself surprised, nor allow himself to be startled. He was also learning to think very quickly, and as soon as Chrissie Walker spoke he remembered that the Cat and Bagpipe was close to Endsleigh Gardens, the place of appointment mentioned in the note which he had picked up on the scene of Alfred Jakyn's death, and that both were within a few minutes' walk of the Euston Hotel. So he merely elevated his eyebrows in a politely inquisitive glance, as if just a little mildly interested.

"Oh!" he said. "That so? You recognize him?"

"Should think I did!" replied Chrissie fervently. "Good-looking fellow, isn't he? Oh, yes, no mistaking that...knew that photo as soon as I set eyes on it. That's the man!"

"And he came in here...Monday night?" asked Jennison.

"Came in here, Monday night...as I say," responded Chrissie, "with a lady. Looked in himself first, through that door, and seeing there was nobody much about...we were very quiet, as usual, at that time...he brought her in. They sat down in that alcove there. Oh, yes!"

"What time would that be?" asked Jennison.

"A bit after ten o'clock," replied Chrissie. "Just about the time when I usually begin to yawn. Five or ten minutes past ten."

"Did they stay long?" inquired Jennison.

"Twenty minutes or so," answered the barmaid. "He'd a couple of whiskey's; she'd a small glass of port...which she scarcely touched: I noticed that. They were talking all the time...confidential talk, it seemed...whispers, you know. It struck me they'd turned in here on purpose to talk. He appeared to be explaining something; he did most of the talking, anyhow."

"Seem to be friendly?" asked Jennison.

"As far as I could see," replied Chrissie. "Quite friendly. I should have said they were talking business. Of course, I didn't catch a word of it. But that's the man, sure as anything!"

"Interesting!" remarked Jennison. "Credit to your powers of observation! And what was the lady like?"

Chrissie laughed and gave her questioner a knowing look.

"Well, I'll tell you," she said, leaning over the counter. "She was a pretty little woman, I should say a bit over thirty...p'raps a year or two more. Dark hair, dark eyes...quite pretty. She'd a big, very plain, but good cloak on that wrapped her right up, and she'd a veil, though not a thick one. But I noticed this...she undid her cloak to get something, a handkerchief or a smelling bottle, or something of that sort, and I saw that she'd got a dinner-dress on, and a very smart one, too! I only saw it for a moment, mind you, but I did see!"

"Ah!" exclaimed Jennison. "Just so! Um!"

"He wasn't in evening dress," continued Chrissie. "He'd a dark suit on...blue serge, I think. And I'll tell you what I thought...I thought she was some lady who'd been dining at one of the big hotels close by, or at one of the houses in one of those big squares at the back here, and that they'd met, and wanted to have a bit of quiet talk, and so they'd turned in here. But fancy it being that man! and his being dead, actually dead and gone...an hour or so after!"

"Life's a very uncertain thing, you know!" answered Jennison with the air of one who utters a solemn truth for the very first time. "That's a fact! Well...I wouldn't mention this to anybody else if I were you, Chrissie! Just keep it to yourself...see?"

"Why?" demanded Chrissie.

"Well, if you like, as a personal favour to me," replied Jennison. "Don't tell anybody else that you saw Alfred Jakyn in here. Leastways, not without telling me. I mean, really, don't tell anybody unless I say you can."

"Why, what've you got to do with it?" asked Chrissie. "No affair of yours, is it?"

Jennison pointed to the newspaper account and to his own name in capitals.

"As the principal witness in the case," he replied loftily, "and as the one person that witnessed...actually witnessed...the unfortunate catastrophe, I should say it is my affair! But between you and me, there's more than that in it. I'm doing a bit in my own way to unravel this mystery...there's more mystery in this business than you'd think, and I should like to keep what you've told me to myself. It may be of...well, what they call supreme importance."

"Oh, well!" said Chrissie, "I don't suppose anybody'll come asking questions at the Cat and Bagpipe. So you want to find things out, do you?"

"You shall know more later," replied Jennison, with a significant look. "In the meantime, be a good girl, and say...nothing! These cases, silence...ah, you don't know what a lot depends on silence...properly applied!"

He drank his bitter beer and went out, to think. So Alfred Jakyn and a lady...veiled, and in evening dress...had been closeted together in a quiet corner of the saloon bar of the Cat and Bagpipe between ten and ten-thirty on the night of his death, had they? Very good! that was a valuable addition to his score of knowledge. Of course, the lady was the writer of the note which he had found; the note making an appointment at the west end of Endsleigh Gardens. That end was within a minute of the Cat and Bagpipe. They had met, these two, and turned in there to talk.

And it was close to the Euston Hotel; and the waiter from the Euston Hotel had said at the inquest that he had seen Alfred Jakyn examine or read a scrap of paper just before leaving the smoking-room. That, said the waiter, was about or close on ten o'clock: well, said Jennison, it would only take a smart walker two or three minutes to walk from the Euston Hotel to the end of Endsleigh Gardens. Um! things were smoothing themselves out; becoming connected: there was a clue. And with the idea of getting a still firmer hold of it, Jennison crossed the Euston Road, made for the big, gloomy portals of the station, and, turning into the hotel, looked for and walked into the smoking-room.

It was a room of considerable dimensions, this, but when Jennison entered it was almost deserted. Two elderly men sat talking in a corner; a younger man was busy at a writing-table. It was with a writing-table that Jennison was first concerned. There were several in the room, placed here and there in convenient corners; he went across to the most isolated, took from his pocket-book the scrap of paper which he had picked up in Cartwright Gardens, and compared it with the hotel letter-paper stored in the stationery rack. It required no more than a glance to assure him that the paper on which the mysterious message had been written was identical in material, color and weight, with that before him. Without doubt, the scrap which he had preserved so carefully, and the existence of which he had kept secret, had been torn from a half-sheet of the Euston Hotel note-paper.

Jennison returned his treasured bit of evidence to his pocket-book, enclosed in a full sheet of the hotel stationery, and leaving the writing-table, went over to a seat in a corner and rang a bell. He hoped that the waiter who had given evidence at the inquest would answer that summons. His hopes were fulfilled: that very man appeared, and what was more, he recognized Jennison at once, and looked at him with unusual curiosity.

"You know me?" suggested Jennison. "Saw me at that inquest, didn't you? I saw you, of course. I say! I want a word or two with you...on the quiet. Get me, say, a bottle of Bass, and when you come back with it...eh?"

The waiter nodded comprehending, and retired. In five minutes he was back again with the Bass, and Jennison opened fire on him without delay.

"Look here!" he said, glancing round to make sure that they had that quarter of the room to themselves. "That affair, now; I'm inquiring into it, and if you can give a bit of help, it'll be something...maybe a good deal...in your pocket. You know what you said before the Coroner? That Alfred Jakyn, the dead man, came into this room about nine-thirty that night...Monday night? To be sure! Well, now, who was in it when he came in?"

The waiter had been considering Jennison. He, too, looked round. And he sank his voice to a pitch that denoted confidential communication.

"You ain't doing this on behalf of the police?" he asked. "Just so! private like...reasons of your own. I see! Well, when Jakyn came in that night, there were only two people in this room...a lady and a gentleman. Together...husband and wife, they were. Staying in the hotel, you know: I'd seen 'em two or three times before; they were here over the week-end; Friday afternoon to Tuesday morning. He was an elderly man; seventy, I should say, by his looks. She was a great deal younger: half his age."

"Who were they?" inquired Jennison.

"Names I can't give you...at present," replied the waiter. "But I can find 'em out in five minutes. Now, if you like."

"Wait a bit...that'll do after," said Jennison. "You say they were in this room when Jakyn came in? What were they doing?"

"The old gentleman was sitting over there, in that chair, smoking a cigar, and reading a magazine. The lady was at that table, close by his chair, writing."

"How was she dressed?"

"Evening dress...dinner dress...they'd turned in here after dinner. He was in a dinner jacket. I'd served 'em with coffee not so long before Jakyn came in...they'd dined rather late."

"What happened after Jakyn came in?"

"Happened? Well, nothing...but that he asked me to get him a whiskey and soda. He was sitting across there; near where the lady was writing."

"Did he seem to know these two...or her—or they, or she, him?"

"Not that I saw of. Took no notice of each other. Can't say, of course, what went on while I was fetching his drink. When I came back with it, they'd gone...the old gentleman and lady and Jakyn was alone."

"And you say...at least, you said at the inquest...that he was a bit restless?"

"Well, he was...in a manner. Walked about the room, you understand...talked to himself a bit...muttered, vaguely; seemed uneasy, upset. And, as I said, I saw him pull out a bit of paper, folded up, unfold it, put it back in his waistcoat pocket when he'd read it, and then..well, he walked out rather sharply after that. As if...well, as if he'd just made up his mind about something or other."

"That was just before ten o'clock, wasn't it?"

"Just before, it would be. Five or ten minutes to ten, I reckon."

"You never saw him again?"

"No! till I saw him at the mortuary. They took me there, you see, after that detective chap had been here."

Jennison had money in his pocket; what was more, he was minded to lay it out. He quietly slipped a couple of pound-notes into the waiter's palm.

"That's to be going on with," he murmured. "You keep this to yourself, and there'll be more...maybe a good deal more...to follow. Now look here, can you get me the names of that elderly gentleman and the lady? And...address?"

"Easy!" replied the waiter. "Two minutes."

He left the room, and Jennison ruminated. He had no doubt, now, after hearing the waiter's story, that when Alfred Jakyn walked into that room on the evening of his death, he had recognized in the lady at the writing-table somebody whom he had known before, and that she had recognized him. Nor had he any doubt that neither of them wished the elderly gentleman to know of the mutual recognition. He fancied that he saw exactly how the thing was done. The lady tore off a scrap of paper from the sheet before her, scribbled a message on it, and either dropped it on the floor near Alfred Jakyn's chair, or placed it in some position after attracting his attention to it. Then she and the old gentleman retired, and probably he went to bed, while she put on a wrap and went out to keep the appointment she had just made.

"That's how it's been worked," mused Jennison. "Fits in like...like one of them jigsaw puzzles. Brains! that's all you want, to put these things together. And I ain't wanting in brains, I believe!"

The waiter came back. He had a bit of paper in his hand, and he laid it before Jennison with a nod. Jennison read what was penciled on it. Sir John and Lady Cheale, Cheale Court, Chester.

"Know who they are?" he asked.

"Not particularly...I'm new to this place," replied the waiter. "The head waiter says they're well known here, though; turn up now and then for a few days. Big pot in the North, the old gentleman, I understand...millionaire, or something."

Then some men came into the room, calling for drinks, and the waiter went off, and Jennison left. He had now two pieces of paper to take care of and he hadn't the slightest doubt that they were closely related. Jennison thought a lot that night. The mystery surrounding the circumstances of Alfred Jakyn's death centered, he felt sure, in Jakyn's meeting with the woman with whom Chrissie Walker had seen him in company at the Cat and Bagpipe; the woman who, if he, Jennison, was putting two and two together accurately, was Lady Cheale. Now, who was Lady Cheale? That, of course, could be found out. But what had she to do with Alfred Jakyn? Were they old acquaintances? Was the meeting at the Euston Hotel an unforeseen, accidental one? And why did the lady fix upon a place outside, a rendezvous well removed from the hotel, though, to be sure, of easy access?

And then another question shaped itself in Jennison's inquisitive mind. Where was Alfred Jakyn between half-past ten and a quarter to twelve on the night of his death? According to Chrissie Walker, he left the Cat and Bagpipe in company with his lady companion at or before 10.30. Where was he until 11.45, when he suddenly appeared in Cartwright Gardens, and fell dead?

"Devil of a lot of things to find out in this affair!" mused Jennison. "One thing at a time, however. And first...Lady Cheale!"

He had some idea that you can find out these things from books...books of reference. What books, he was dimly uncertain about, but still books. And next day, when his luncheon hour came round in the city, he went to a reference library, and began to search. Jennison's notions of titled folks were very vague; he thought he should find Sir John Cheale's name in the Peerage, and was astonished that he didn't. Nor was he in the Baronetage...which, in Jennison's opinion, was still more astonishing. Eventually he asked a librarian to help him: the librarian suggested Who's Who. And there Jennison got light. Sir John Cheale, son of John Cheale, of Manchester. Born 1850. Educated Shrewsbury School and Trinity College, Cambridge. Knighted 1918. Principal partner and chairman of directors of Cheale & Company, Ltd., chemical manufacturers, Chester.

Deputy-Lieutenant for the County of Cheshire. Married, 1918, Mildred, daughter of the late William Colebrooke, of Cheltenham: no issue. Collector of books, pictures, antiques. Clubs: Grosvenor, Chester; and Constitutional, London.

Residences: Cheale Court, Chester, and Ardrechan, Braemar, Scotland. Before he had got to the last word in this informing paragraph, Jennison had made up his mind to go down to Chester and waylay Lady Cheale: Lady Cheale meant...money.

Chapter 6

Jennison's notions as to precisely how Lady Cheale meant money were vague, shapeless, but they were there. To carry them out, or to make a beginning in the process of carrying them out, or attempting to carry them out, he had no objection to spending money of his own, and next morning he drew funds from his savings. Nobody, reflected Jennison, can expect to make money unless they lay out money. That done, he sought the presence of the manager of the warehouse, and pulled a long face, at the same time indicating the lump on his face.

"Got to have that off tomorrow," he said lugubriously. "Operation! The doctor says I ought to have had it done before. Serious business, as it's been neglected. Might be some danger about it, too...strict quiet and rest are necessary anyway after the operation. I shall have to take a bit of time off."

"How long?" asked the manager.

"He said, a few days, at least, the doctor," replied Jennison. "Depends! Shock to the system, you know."

The manager didn't know, and he glanced at Jennison's lump.

"It certainly does seem as if it had grown a bit," he remarked. "Well, we aren't particularly busy; you'd better take a week. If that's not enough, you can write and ask for another. Put you under chloroform, I suppose, eh?"

"He didn't say," answered Jennison, still affecting melancholy. "I reckon he will, of course. Beastly nuisance! Still, one's got to get it over."

But he had no intention of getting it over: none whatever of going near Dr. Syphax and the surgery in Brunswick Square: his plans were far otherwise. And when he left the warehouse at noon he turned into the nearest public telephone box, and ringing up Dr. Syphax, canceled the appointment for next morning, saying that urgent business compelled him to put off the operation for a day or two...he would call, later, and fix things. That done, he went home to Cartwright Gardens, arrayed himself in his best clothes, packed a small suit-case, and, repairing to Euston, ate a hearty lunch at the refreshment bar, and caught the next train to Chester. As the autumn afternoon drew to an end, he was walking the streets of that ancient town, fully alive to the delights of his adventure.

Jennison knew nothing about that corner of England, and cared less; its sole attraction to him lay in the fact that Lady Cheale, who, he was convinced, was an important factor in the Alfred Jakyn affair, lived in it, somewhere. He could not, of course, find her that night, but he knew how to make inquiries about her. He came off country-town stock himself, and knew where, in country towns, you can always get hold of information. And though...being minded to be comfortable...he put himself up at a good hotel, and ate his dinner there, he took good care not to spend his evening in its highly-respectable purlieus. You don't find gossips nor local talk in places like that, said Jennison, knowingly: they're all very well to sleep in and eat in, but if you want to know things about a town and its people you must frequent a good old-fashioned tavern where tradesmen go when the day's business is done, to enjoy pipe and glass, and pass the time of day. And when Jennison had dined, he sent out to find such a tavern, and had no difficulty in his search, every ancient English city and market town possessing an almost puzzling wealth of resorts of that nature.

The house into which Jennison turned was a quaint, old-world place, wherein was a big, roomy bar-parlor, furnished with antique, worm-eaten, highly polished chairs, tables, and long settles, ornamented with old glass, brass, copper, sporting pictures, pictures of stage-coach days, and playbills of the era of the Kembles, to say nothing of a fire big enough for the roasting of an ox. Jennison got himself into a comfortable, snug corner, ordered a drink, and observed things. There were several men in the room, all obviously regular customers. Jennison listened to their conversation. It was all about local matters; local politics; local money affairs; local horse racing; local trade; he knew, from his own experiences of his own native place in another part of the country, that every man in that room would be as well up in local knowledge as he would be ignorant of anything outside his own little world. He knew, too, that before the evening was over he would get into conversation with one or other of these men, and would find out all he wanted to know. And that was easy when a middle-aged man dropped into a chair alongside his own, remarked that it was a cold night outside and warm enough in there, and fell, bit by bit, into friendly talk. Jennison, artful and designing, led the way to talk of local trades and industries, letting his neighbor know that he was a stranger.

"Lot of big chemical works hereabouts, aren't there?" suggested Jennison. "Sort of principal industry, isn't it?"

"Considerable lot of 'em in the district," assented his companion. "Chemicals...soap...iron...coal...that sort of thing. Big affairs, you know...employ a lot of labor."

"Isn't there a big chemical works called Cheale's?" inquired Jennison. "I'm interested in chemical works, indirectly."

"Cheale's? Oh, yes!" replied the other. "Yes, one of the biggest industries hereabouts. Flourishing concern, that; they do say that Sir John Cheale, the principal shareholder...founder, he was, originally...is a multi-millionarie!"

"Local man?" asked Jennison.

That question set the informant off. In a few minutes Jennison knew all about Sir John Cheale, the big business, and where Sir John Cheale lived. Cheale Court was a fine old house a few miles out of Chester, in the country. Nearest village, Wilsmere: nice walk out there. Wilsmere belonged to Sir John, and it was a model village, worth going to see.

Great collector of books and pictures, Sir John was; they did say that he'd one of the finest private libraries in England, and his pictures were famous...these old masters and that sort of thing. Been an old bachelor, Sir John had, most of his life, but lately...well, within the last year or two...had married. Rare pretty bit of womankind, too! deal younger than he was...oh, yes, quite a young woman. Not of these parts, Lady Cheale...no, Sir John married her while he was away somewhere—caused a good deal of surprise when he brought her home. Often to be seen in Chester, Lady Cheale...came in a good deal in her motor-car...smart little woman, Lady Cheale! Jennison took it all in, determining that he would see Lady Cheale closer at hand. He contrived to get hold of a map of the district that night, and before he went to bed, and by diligently studying it, made out that the village of Wilsmere, of which his informant had spoken, was only three or four miles from Chester, and that Cheale Court was on its immediate confines. Arguing that Lady Cheale probably attended the services at Wilsmere Church, he determined, the next day being Sunday, to walk out there in the morning, and see if he could get a glimpse of her. And if he did...

Next morning, then, Jennison, looking for all the world like an innocent, well-dressed young gentleman, presented himself as a stranger at the church door of Wilsmere, and was duly shown to a seat. He was very well-behaved and quite devout, but his eyes saw without seeming to see, and before the officiating clergyman had said many words of the service, Jennison was certain that there, in a sort of family pew close by his own seat, was the woman described by Chrissie Walker. She was now in far different surroundings, and in the purple and fine linen befitting her position as wife of the great local magnate, but Jennison felt instinctively that if the barmaid of the Cat and Bagpipe had been at his side she would have lost little time in nudging his elbow and whispering, regardless of grammatical rule, that...that...was...her!

He had no doubt about Lady Cheale's identity when the service was over and he got a still closer look at her near the church porch. Dark hair dark eyes...pretty, taking...not much over thirty, if that...bet your life, swore Jennison, this is the woman! Nor had he any possibility of doubting that this woman was Lady Cheale. Although this is the twentieth century, there are villages in England where the squire's lady is still somebody, and the pretty woman who passed down the churchyard path had her due meed of obeisance and curtsy from the rustics who lined it. A great personage in her own parish, Lady Cheale, evidently! but never mind, said Jennison; he knew things that would bring haughtier and grander folk than Lady Cheale to their knees...perhaps to his knees!

Instead of returning to Chester, Jennison sought out the village inn, and got a midday dinner there. Later, he lounged round Wilsmere and took a look at Cheale Court, a fine old

Elizabethan house set in the midst of a big park. And finding that there were public paths through the park, he took one that led him near the house, and suddenly as he turned the corner of a shrubbery, he came face to face with the woman of whom he was thinking. Lady Cheale, evidently, was out for a constitutional in her own extensive grounds, and she was alone, save for the presence of a couple of fox terriers, who, at sight of Jennison, rushed forward barking. Their mistress called them off.

"Come here, Wasp! come here, Smiler! come here! They won't harm you!" she added to Jennison, smilingly. "They're quite safe, they don't bite..."

Jennison lifted his hat, in his best manner.

"I'm not afraid of dogs," he said. "Been used to them all my life." In token of his indifference, he snapped his fingers at the fox terriers, chirruping at them with pursed lips. And as they grew quiet, sniffing around his shoes, he looked steadily at the pretty woman now close to him, and again raised his hat. "Lady Cheale, I believe?" he inquired politely.

Lady Cheale looked a little surprised, and took stock of her questioner. Jennison was quite a presentable young man, even when judged by a high standard; Lady Cheale bowed in response to his question.

"May I have a word or two with your ladyship?" continued Jennison. He looked round, and seeing no one anywhere in sight, and that they were in a lonely part of the park, pressed his advantage. "The fact is, I came down from London specially, last night, to see you, Lady Cheale. But this seems a good opportunity...if you'll listen to me."

Lady Cheale, too, glanced around her. There was some slight alarm, more wonder, in her eyes when she turned again to Jennison. But he looked harmless enough. Still, Jennison saw a slight paling of her cheek.

"To see me?" she exclaimed. "I...I don't know you! I saw you in church this morning...a stranger to the village. Who...who are you? And why..."

Jennison nodded.

"Yes," he said quietly. "Of course you'll want to know that, Lady Cheale. But I think you'll know my name well enough when you hear it. No doubt you're quite familiar with it. For I'm sure you've read the reports in the newspapers about the inquest on Alfred Jakyn!"

There was no doubt then about the change of color in Lady Cheale's pretty face. The healthy glow on her cheeks died out, was extinguished, came back just as suddenly in a vivid flood. A startled, frightened look flashed into her eyes; her lips trembled.

"Who...who are you?" she faltered, moving a little away. "Why do you come here? Are you a...a detective?"

"No!" answered Jennison. "I said you'd know my name, Lady Cheale. And please don't be afraid...there's nothing to be afraid about. My name is Jennison...Albert Jennison. I'm the man who witnessed Alfred Jakyn's death!"

Lady Cheale stood watching Jennison, for the better part of a moment, in silence. Jennison, on his part, watched her. Her colour was becoming normal; her eyes suspicious rather than afraid; he saw that she was taking guard against whatever might be coming.

"Of course you read the account of the inquest, Lady Cheale," he continued. "You'll remember my evidence. I'm the man who, from my window in Cartwright Gardens, saw Alfred Jakyn, walking on the pavement in apparently the very best of health, suddenly collapse and fall. It was I who ran down to him and found him dead...only just dead, but as dead as if he'd been dead a hundred years. But you know all that, you've read it in the newspapers. Haven't you, Lady Cheale?"

Lady Cheale was still watching him fixedly. She made no answer to his question; instead she put a question herself, in a hard, dry voice.

"Why have you come here to see me?"

Jennison smiled, for the first time. It was a smile that Lady Cheale did not like; it suggested unpleasant possibilities.

"I'll tell you, Lady Cheale. I came here to ask you what you know about Alfred Jakyn! Just that!"

Once again there was an interchange of straight, questioning glances. When Lady Cheale spoke, her voice was harder than before.

"How do you know that I know anything about Alfred Jakyn?" she demanded.

Jennison once more looked round. But they were alone; the house lay a mile away among the trees; not a soul was in sight. The fox terriers had left their mistress to nose round a rabbit-warren.

"I suppose we can talk here as well as within four walls," observed Jennison, "perhaps better, with more safety. I'll tell you, Lady Cheale, now I know that you know something...perhaps a good deal...about Alfred Jakyn. I've taken an interest in this case from the moment in which I found Alfred Jakyn dead: all the greater interest because, do you see, I'd seen him alive and lively as a man can be, only two or three minutes before. And I determined to find things out...to get at the bottom of the mystery which I felt certain was there. I wanted to...know! And there are certain things I know already..."

"What do you know about me?" interrupted Lady Cheale sharply. "Something...real or imaginary! or you wouldn't be here! What now?"

Jennison looked her straight and hard in the face.

"I know that you were with Alfred Jakyn during the evening on which he died, Lady Cheale!" he answered. "That's what!"

Lady Cheale bit her lips, in obvious perplexity. A slight pucker appeared between the delicate arch of her eyebrows; she seemed to be thinking, to be endeavoring to recall something. Suddenly she snapped out another question.

"How do you know that?" she demanded. "Perhaps you know something, but..."

Jennison stopped her with another of the confident smiles she did not like.

"Look here, Lady Cheale," he said, "I'm the sort of player that'll lay his cards on the table. I'm quite willing to lay mine before you. So, listen! At ten o'clock of the evening on which Alfred Jakyn met his death, you met him at the west-end corner of Endsleigh Gardens. You and he went into the saloon-bar of the Cat and Bagpipe tavern, close by. You remained there about half an hour, in close conversation, in an alcove. Then you left, going away together. Lady Cheale, that's...fact!"

He looked at her with a certain air of triumph, as if expecting her to throw up the sponge. But Lady Cheale shook her head.

"You may have acquired some information," she said, slowly, "but you've no proof..."

"Oh!" exclaimed Jennison. "There you're wrong, Lady

Cheale! Proof!"

And this time laughing gently, instead of smiling, he drew out of his pocket, and held unfolded before her, the scrap of paper which he had found in Cartwright Gardens and had treasured so carefully ever since.

Chapter 7

For the second time during their interview, Jennison saw Lady Cheale's color sweep clear away from her cheeks. Her face grew drawn and tense, and her lips parted involuntarily as she stared at the crumpled sheet of paper which Jennison held up to her. And when she spoke, her voice came in a husky whisper. Jennison knew, hearing that whisper, that at last she was thoroughly frightened.

"Where...where did you get that?" she faltered. "Where? How?"

Jennison carefully folded the paper and restored it to its usual resting place in his pocket.

"I said I was the sort to put all my cards on the table, Lady Cheale," he replied, slowly. "I'm going to be as good as my word. But first...you know that's your writing on that paper? Isn't it, now?"

"Well?" she muttered. "Well?"

"Of course it is!" exclaimed Jennison cheerfully, as if he were emphasizing some joyous announcement. "We both know that! Very well, how did I get it? I'll tell you, Lady Cheale. You know already that I was the only person who witnessed the death of Alfred Jakyn. The police came...on my summons. I went with them to the mortuary, I saw and heard all that took place there; the police surgeon hinted at foul play; I knew he meant poison. I accompanied a detective, Womersley, to make inquiries of Bradmore, whose card had been found on the dead man's body. Then I went home, alone. As I reached the spot at which Alfred Jakyn fell, I saw a piece of twisted paper lying in the gutter where he'd lain. I picked it up and took it to my room...it was the piece of paper I've just shown you."

He paused, as if expecting Lady Cheale to speak. But Lady Cheale said nothing; she was watching him, steadily, expectantly. And Jennison went on, in the same level tones, watching her as steadily as she watched him.

"I saw that the handwriting was a woman's, and I felt certain the piece of paper had been given to Alfred Jakyn by some woman. But I kept the knowledge to myself. I said nothing of my discovery to the police; I said nothing about it when I gave evidence at the inquest. Lady Cheale...if it's any relief to you, there isn't a soul in the world knows that I found and that I have that paper...written by you!"

A whisper came from Lady Cheale's compressed lips.

"No one?"

"No one!" assented Jennison. "As I say, not a soul in the world! It's never been out of my possession; nobody's seen it; I've never mentioned it to anybody: nobody has the least suspicion that I have it, or that there was ever such a document for anybody to have! Get that firmly impressed on your mind, Lady Cheale. But...how did I connect you with it? Because this is a much smaller world than people think! On the evening of the inquest, Lady Cheale, a portrait of Alfred Jakyn appeared in one or two of the evening newspapers. I handed one such paper to the barmaid of the Cat and Bagpipe: she immediately exclaimed that the man whose portrait was there had been in her saloon bar on Monday night, with a lady. I showed no surprise: I let her talk. She described the lady; she gave me the facts. When I left her, I'd put two-and-two together, and I went across to the Euston Hotel. Alfred Jakyn had put up there...and I believed that it was there that the note I had found had been handed to him."

Once more Jennison paused. But Lady Cheale made no comment. The color had come back to her cheeks again, but the unusual brightness of her eyes and her quick breathing betrayed her suppressed excitement. She was waiting to know all, and Jennison realized it.

"I went to the Euston Hotel," he continued. "I examined the hotel note-paper in the stationery stands in the smoking-room. I saw at once that the note in my possession was written on a piece of paper that had been torn from a sheet of the hotel stuff: there was no doubt about that. Then I got hold of the waiter who had given evidence at the inquest as to Alfred Jakyn having been in the smoking-room from about nine-thirty to close on ten that Monday night. He told me, privately, of certain facts. A lady was writing at a table when Alfred Jakyn entered; an elderly gentleman sat near, reading a periodical: the waiter left Alfred Jakyn with these two while he went to get him a drink. When he returned, the lady and elderly gentleman had gone. Alfred Jakyn seemed excited, or perturbed; he wandered about the room; he seemed to be thinking; finally he consulted a piece of paper which he took from his pocket, and just before ten he went hurriedly away. Now, Lady Cheale, it didn't take many minutes to find out who the elderly gentleman and the lady were, and I found out. Sir John Cheale and Lady Cheale, of Cheale Court. You, Lady Cheale, and your husband...who probably suspects nothing!"

Jennison threw a peculiar emphasis on his last words, and he saw Lady Cheale start and the color deepen in her cheeks. She gave Jennison an angry look.

"Leave Sir John Cheale out of it!" she said.

"With pleasure," answered Jennison. "I hope he may never come into it. But...what have you to say to me, Lady Cheale? It was you, you know, who wrote that note to Alfred Jakyn; you who either slipped it into his hand or dropped it near him as you left the smoking-room; you who met him a short time afterwards at the west corner of Endsleigh Gardens; you who went with him into the saloon-bar of the Cat and Bagpipe. Now why?"

"What's that got to do with you?" demanded Lady Cheale. "What business is it of yours? What..."

Jennison stopped her with a look and tapped the breast of his smart overcoat.

"Don't forget that I've got that bit of paper in here, Lady Cheale!" he said warning. "If I hand it over to the police..."

Lady Cheale's momentary flash of anger changed to a look of sullenness.

"What?" she asked resentfully.

"Goodness knows!" answered Jennison, with a deep sigh. "But that chap Womersley, who has this case in hand, and who firmly believes that Alfred Jakyn was murdered, by poison, is one of those fellows who don't allow sentiment to interfere with their professional duties. Hard chap! I think. He's not like me. I'd hate to cause pain or annoyance to a lady. Especially," he added, with a grimace and a bow, "to a young and charming one, Lady Cheale!"

Lady Cheale's lips curled.

"How can I rely on your word that you've never told any

one of this?" she asked, almost contemptuously. "I mean...of that note?"

"You can believe me or not, as you please," retorted Jennison, quietly. "But it's a positive fact that I haven't. I repeat...nobody knows anything about it!"

Lady Cheale looked down on the path on which they were standing, and began to make holes in its gravelly surface with the point of her walking-stick. She was evidently thinking, and Jennison knew she was, and he waited.

"Well," she said at last, still looking down, "I did meet Alfred Jakyn. I knew him...some time ago. I wanted to discuss a business matter with him...privately. But I know nothing whatever about the cause of his death...nothing! And I do not want my name to be dragged into any proceedings. I don't want to be brought into the affair at all!"

"Of course not, Lady Cheale!" said Jennison heartily. "Of course not! That's precisely why I came down here to see you. Remember, you only could be drawn in through me!"

"That barmaid?" suggested Lady Cheale.

"She knows nothing of the note and never will," asserted Jennison. "And it's a million to one against her ever setting eyes on you again!"

"The waiter?" she asked.

"He, too, knows nothing of the note," replied Jennison. "And, of course,
he hasn't the slightest suspicion that anything occurred between you and Alfred Jakyn. The note, Lady Cheale, the note is the thing! And that it exists at all will never be known to anybody if..."

Jennison stopped. He knew now, had known ever since an early stage of the conversation, what he was really after, but he had still some diffidence that was really akin to a constitutional delicacy of feeling in actually saying it.

"If...what?" asked Lady Cheale.

"Well, if...if you and I could come to an understanding...terms, you know," he answered. "It's a...a secret! And secrets are worth...something!"

Lady Cheale gave him a calm, searching look.

"You want money?" she asked quietly.

"I could do with money," answered Jennison. Then, gathering courage, he added. "You see, Lady Cheale, it's this way. I'm a clerk. A clerk in a London warehouse...been there years...dull, dreary years! In reality, though I'm pretty well paid, as things go, I hate it! I want adventure! I want to travel, to see things...abroad..."

Lady Cheale interrupted him, almost eagerly.

"You'd go abroad? if you had money?"

"I would do!" exclaimed Jennison.

"At once?"

"As soon as...yes, it would be at once. Immediately...nothing to stop me."

Lady Cheale hesitated a moment and then took a step nearer to Jennison.

"Listen!" she said. "If I give you money, will you hand over that piece of paper to me, and give me your solemn word that you'll never speak a word of all this as long as you live?"

"I will!" exclaimed Jennison. "Honor bright!"

"What part of the world are you thinking of?" asked Lady Cheale.

"Oh!" said Jennison, almost rapturously. "If you want to know that...Italy! The fact is, Lady Cheale, I'm poetic! If I could have a year or two in Italy, and perhaps in Greece..."

"Listen to me again," said Lady Cheale. "On the conditions I've laid down, I'll find you in money. You give me that paper, you hold your tongue, and you leave England at once. I'll give you a thousand pounds in cash, and I'll send you another thousand on hearing from you that you have an address in, say, Rome."

"Done! and immensely, greatly obliged to you, Lady Cheale," exclaimed Jennison. "I hope, I sincerely hope, you'll feel I've done you some little service? I'll keep my part of the bargain to the letter, and I assure you..."

"I don't want any protestation, if you please," interrupted Lady Cheale icily. "This is a business matter. Now, are you staying in Chester? Very well...tomorrow morning, about eleven o'clock, go into Bolland's, the confectioners; everybody knows Bolland's. Go upstairs to the tea-rooms and sit down in a quiet corner and order a cup of coffee. I shall come to you there and that's all!"

Before Jennison could say another word, she had turned, whistled to her dogs, and marched swiftly away. And Jennison watched her for a minute or two before he went off...and his first thought was not one of elation, but of regret, that Lady Cheale hadn't said good-bye to him.

"She...might...have shaken hands with me!" he murmured, as he watched Lady Cheale's graceful figure out of sight. "By George, sir, she's a damn fine woman! a prettier woman than I'd expected. And...two thousand pounds! Her own terms! Generous! And it means that she doesn't want her name to come out, anyhow. Well, it won't! Not me! with two thousand pounds and Italy and Greece in front. And all because of a scrap of paper!"

He walked back to Chester in a whirl of jumbled ideas. Of course, there was going to be no more warehouse; he'd chuck that without ever going back there; there'd be nothing to do but resign his post. And he'd take no further interest in the Cartwright Gardens affair; indeed, so that Womersley and the police couldn't come worrying him about it, he'd leave his present lodgings and go elsewhere, somewhere in a more fashionable part, say a West End hotel or boarding-house, until he went abroad, and he'd forget to leave any address with his old landlady. Of course, he couldn't go abroad immediately: he'd want an outfit, and he'd have to consider where to go first. Well, it was certainly an ill wind that blew nobody any good, and if that eventful Monday midnight had brought death, swift and sudden, to Alfred Jakyn, it had also brought good fortune to yours truly, Albert Jennison...rather! Two thousand of the best! The figure, fat, rotund, impressive, shaped itself before him in the midst of rose-tinted clouds all the way to Chester, and during the whole of the evening, and when he retired to bed, he dreamed of it.

Eleven o'clock next morning found Jennison in a quiet corner of the fashionable tea-shop which Lady Cheale had mentioned, and there, a few minutes later, Lady Cheale, very elegant in expensive furs, joined him. Everything about her manner that morning betokened a business-like attitude, and after a greeting which Jennison considered unnecessarily chilly, she went straight to the point.

"You have that note with you?" she demanded.

"Precisely so, Lady Cheale!" replied Jennison. "In my pocket-book, where it's always been."

"You can hand it to me in a few minutes, and I will give you the promised money, in bank-notes," she said. "But first, a question or two." She leaned nearer to him across the tea-tray which had just been put before her. "Can you tell me this...have the police, has that detective you spoke of yesterday afternoon, found out anything more about Alfred Jakyn?"

"Not to my knowledge," declared Jennison promptly.

"You have heard nothing of that sort?"

"Nothing!"

"Another question. Do you know whether they have had any news of him, or concerning him, from New York?"

"I don't know that, either."

"I read in the papers that there was a bank draft for some thousands of dollars found in his suit-case, payable to an American bank in the city. Do you know if the police made any inquiries there?"

Jennison smiled, and lowered his voice, though, as a matter of fact, no one was near them.

"I don't know!" he answered. "But I did!"

"You?" she exclaimed.

"Yes...out of curiosity. They knew nothing whatever about him."

Lady Cheale hesitated a moment. Then she leaned still nearer.

"Do you know if the police have found out where he was between ten-thirty and eleven-thirty that Monday night?" she asked.

"No, by George!" exclaimed Jennison. "I don't! I believe they've found out nothing...I'm sure they haven't. I wish I knew that particular thing...where he was, at that time."

"You!" she said. "You have nothing to do with it...now! You are to take no further interest in it...you're to know nothing. Now, give me that paper!"

Jennison handed over the treasured scrap, and Lady Cheale having carefully examined it and put it in her bag, gave him an envelope full of crisp bank-notes.

"That is the first installment I promised you," she said. "Send me an address in Rome, and the second will be sent to you at once. And now...silence! That's all...you'd better go away...I'm staying here awhile."

Jennison felt himself dismissed. He had to go, and he saw that his polite adieu were not wanted. He turned and looked back when he had reached the door of the room...Lady

Cheale was calmly pouring out her tea and had not even a glance for him.

"And yet I ain't such a bad-looking fellow, either!" mused Jennison. "And I've done her a good turn! These high-and-mighties! manners like icebergs. However, the money's all right. And now for Italy...eh!"

He went back to his hotel, and in the privacy of his bedroom counted his bank-notes. Then he packed his suit-case, paid his bill, and went away. Instead of going straight back to London, he traveled across country to his native place, and spent a day or two there, swaggering. He told all and sundry that he had just had a stroke of luck...-done a wonderful deal...business deal...but nobody got any particulars from him. Eventually he started out for London again and within five minutes of getting into his express found himself staring at two big black headlines in the morning newspaper:

> The Cartwright Gardens Mystery:
> Sensational Development!

Chapter 8

It was characteristic of Jennison that before reading further he glanced at his fellow-passengers. There were only two of them: smart-looking, keen-faced men. Some indefinable quality in their appearance made him think them to be connected with the law...solicitors or barristers. Inspecting them more closely, his conviction was strengthened; in the rack above one man reposed one of those curious bags...this one colored red...of the material called repp, in which barristers carry their wigs, gowns, and papers; on the seat by the side of the other was one of those long, narrow, leather valises known as brief bags. Jennison, as a commercial man, knew these things by sight; clearly, their owners were limbs of the law, and he looked them over more narrowly still. But neither took any notice of Jennison: each man was deep in his newspaper. And Jennison turned to his, and beneath the staring headlines which had already caught his attention, read what followed, in bold conspicuous type, double-leaded, and here and there set in capitals or italics:

"We have received the following communication from the authorities at Scotland Yard, with a request to give it a prominent place in our issue of this morning:

'THE COMMISSIONER OF POLICE received, on Monday, by cable from New York, a request from the =President of the Western Lands Development Corporation of Northern America to cable him at once information as to the details in the case of ALFRED JAKYN, who died suddenly in CARTWRIGHT GARDENS, LONDON, about midnight, on October 25, and whose death is believed to have been caused by poison. This information was duly cabled to the inquirer, and the following reply has just been received:

"'President, Western Lands Development Corporation of Northern America, to Commissioner of Police, New Scotland Yard, London. Your information concerning death of Alfred Jakyn duly received. Jakyn was sent over to London by us on secret financial mission of utmost importance. We believe him to have been murdered in order to prevent this being carried out or even begun. We consider critical questions to be settled are: Where was he, and with what person or persons, between ten o'clock and eleven forty-five o'clock on evening of his death? We will pay five thousand pounds to any one giving accurate information to your police on these points. Please communicate this offer to every principal London and English Provincial newspaper. Our accredited representative leaves on personal investigation by today's boat for Southampton.'"

"Any person or persons able to give information on the points referred to above should communicate personally with the authorities at New Scotland Yard, or at ANY POLICE STATION."

Jennison read all this over two or three times, considering it. One part of it stood out from all the rest...to him. *We will pay five thousand pounds to any one giving accurate information to your police!* well, he was the person, he only, who could give such information. But he already had a thousand pounds in his pocket, received on account from Lady Cheale, who was to send him another thousand. He began to wonder which would be the most profitable cow to milk...Lady Cheale, who, to be sure, was the wife of an enormously wealthy man, a millionaire or a multi-millionaire, and who, obviously enough, had some reason for keeping her name out of this affair, or this American financial company with the long name?

Yet, if he approached the police with the idea of getting the five thousand pounds reward, could he tell enough? Would they, or this chap who was already on the Atlantic on his way to make personal investigation, consider his information sufficient? For, after all, he said to himself, he knew a lot, but he didn't know everything...worse luck! He knew where Alfred Jakyn was between ten o'clock and ten-thirty: he was with Lady Cheale at the 'Cat and Bagpipe.' But where was he between ten-thirty and eleven-thirty? If he only knew that...One of his fellow-passengers threw down his paper and glanced at the other.

"Queer development in that Cartwright Gardens affair!" he remarked. "This American company seems remarkably keen about getting a solution. A reward like that...five thousand pounds...ought to bring somebody forward."

But the other man shook his head.

"Doubtful!" he said. "If Jakyn really was poisoned...murdered...for the reason they suggest in their cablegram, it would almost certainly be done in such a fashion that no one but the people concerned would know anything of it."

"Just so, but he must have been somewhere...somewhere in London...between the times mentioned," replied the first man. "I read the account of the inquest carefully, for it's a deeply interesting case. Alfred Jakyn left the Euston Hotel smoking-room just before ten o'clock, according to the evidence of the waiter on duty in that room. Nothing more is known of him until he falls dead in Cartwright Gardens an hour and three-quarters or so later. He must have been somewhere in the interval!"

"I, too, read the evidence," answered the second man. "The waiter said that Jakyn left the smoking-room; he didn't say that he left the hotel. Jakyn may have gone to another part of the hotel to meet somebody with whom he'd an appointment. Hotels are favorite places for business meetings. Why haven't the police made some inquiry as to his movements in the hotel?"

"They may have, for anything we know," observed the first man. "Anyhow, it's certain he was outside the hotel, and, according to the evidence of the witness who saw him fall and die, marching right away from it, just before midnight. No! I think he left the hotel when he left the smoking-room. And in any case, the senders of the cablegram have got the bull by the horns...the thing to be discovered is...where and with whom was Alfred Jakyn between ten and eleven forty-five that evening? That's it!"

"More may come out at the adjourned inquest," remarked the second man. "That's about due, I think."

"It was yesterday," said the first man, nodding towards his paper. "It's in this paper...you'll find it in yours. Nothing much...except that the experts are convinced that the man was poisoned, only they're not quite certain by what. Another adjournment, of course."

The second man picked up his own newspaper and began to search. So, too, after a while did Jennison. The adjourned inquest! He had completely forgotten that: he had fully meant to attend it. But he found, on turning to the report, that he had not missed much. The proceedings had been brief, and entirely confined to hearing some cautious, guarded statements, or, more strictly speaking, suggestions or theories, by a Home Office analyst, who said that he and his colleagues were satisfied that Alfred Jakyn died from the effects of poison, but what poison, and when administered, they were not yet prepared to say.

"There's one thing very certain, to my mind, in this case," suddenly remarked the man who had just picked up the paper to read the account of the adjourned inquest for himself. "And it's this...whoever poisoned Alfred Jakyn was no ordinary criminal! He's an adept at this sort of thing! You can see...for all the scientific jargon he talked...that this Home Office expert is puzzled. So, no doubt, are his associates. Otherwise, they'd say, straight out, what it was."

"Some poison they're not familiar with, either in nature or effect," observed the other. "I dare say there are plenty that our best men don't know of. Queer case altogether...but there must be people in London who saw Alfred Jakyn between ten and eleven forty-five that evening...must!"

Jennison listened to all this and wondered what his fellow-passengers would say if he told them all he knew. It was a temptation to manifest his importance and his cleverness, but he had no difficulty in withstanding it; silence and secretiveness might mean a fortune, and certainly meant at least another thousand. He sat in his corner planning and scheming, and by the time his train ran into the London terminus he had settled his future, and immediate, action. The American cablegram, of course, had altered everything, and now he was either going to have that five thousand pounds out of its senders, or he was going to have it from Lady Cheale.

The most careful and astute of schemers is liable to forget some small point in his plotting, and Jennison, crafty as he was, overlooked a certain thing completely. As soon as he reached London he ought to have gone straight to the Cat and Bagpipe and seen Miss Chrissie Walker. But he forgot Chrissie. Instead of repairing to her presence, he left his suit-case in the luggage office, hired a taxi-cab, and drove down to the city warehouse in which he had spent so many weary days. The manager stared at him: there was a new air about Jennison.

"Hallo!" said the manager. "Got it over?"

Jennison wondered for half a minute what his questioner meant. Then he remembered the lump on his forehead.

"Not yet," he answered. "There's some complication...the doctor says it'll have to be put off a bit. No...I came down to tell you...well, that I'm not coming back!"

"Not coming back?" exclaimed the manager. "Chucking your job? a good job like that! What's this mean?"

"Fact is," replied Jennison, lying glibly now that he had fairly addressed himself to the task, "I've come into money. Unexpected, you know...death of distant relation."

"Oh!" said the manager. "Lucky chap! Much?"

"Fair lot, thank you," answered Jennison. "Enough to chuck this, anyhow!"

"Well," observed the manager, "you know best. But you were about due for another rise, you know. And a job like this...a permanency...eh? However, as I say, you're best judge. Don't go making ducks and drakes of your money now!"

"You bet!" said Jennison. "I know how to take care of money as well as anybody. Ought to!...after making a small screw go as far as I've done, all these years! No! I shan't make ducks and drakes of it, not I!"

"What are you going to do?" asked the manager inquisitively.

"I'm going to travel," declared Jennison. "Improve my mind, you know. I'm leaving England at once. France first, I think...get a knowledge of the language and of commercial matters across there. Then, if I come back, I might go in for something big."

"Well, good luck!" said the manager. "Of course, if you're going in for that sort of thing...languages, foreign correspondence, and so on...you might keep in touch with us. That line's always useful."

Jennison said he'd certainly consider that, if necessary,

in the future. He collected a few things of his own left in his desk, said farewell to his fellow-clerks, and went away. And from the city he drove off to Cartwright Gardens, and there told his landlady another tale, varying somewhat from that he had spun to the manager. The legacy from a relation figured in it, but now he was going to get married and take up his residence at a nice little place in the country, near his native village, which formed part of the legacy. He gave the landlady a couple of pounds in lieu of a week's notice, and proceeded to pack his belongings. That did not occupy much of his time, for they were few, and went easily into a couple of old trunks. And with these Jennison presently made his departure from Cartwright Gardens, saying to himself as he drove away that it wouldn't bother him greatly if he never stuck his face inside that dreary neighborhood again.

He was working on his plan now, and in pursuance of it he went back to the railway station where he had deposited his suit-case, and reclaiming it and adding it to his trunks, bade the driver take him to a certain depository in the Tottenham Court Road district. At that he left the trunks, saying that he was going abroad for a time, and wished them stored. That accomplished, he repaired to a smart outfitting shop, purchased another suit-case, and stored in it a stock of necessaries in the way of linen, footwear, neck-wear, and the like. He was already wearing his best suit, almost brand-new, a new overcoat, and a new hat; he knew himself to be thoroughly presentable. And early in the afternoon he drove up, accompanied by his two suit-cases, to the Great Western Hotel, at Paddington, carefully chosen for reasons which he had resolved on after much thought, and booked a room in the name of Arthur Jennings.

Jennison stayed no longer in that room than was necessary to unpack his suit-cases and make things tidy. He went down to the smoking-room when this was done, and, seating himself at a writing-table, gave himself up to serious consideration of an idea that had been simmering in his brain all the morning. After some time and much cogitation, during which he scribbled meaningless diagrams on the blotting-pad before him, he came to a decision and wrote the following letter:

"DEAR MADAM, You have no doubt already seen the

paragraph in the newspapers relating to the affair which you and I recently discussed. I think you will admit that the offer made in that announcement makes a considerable difference as regards the arrangements I made with you. In view of the much more advantageous terms therein made, I think you will agree that it would pay me far better to place my services at the disposal of these people than remain tied to the terms settled between you and me. Of course, if I had known that these people were going to offer such handsome terms, I should have placed my information before them instead of before you. I feel sure, however, that you will not wish to stand in my light, and that you will be anxious to discuss fresh terms with me. This, of course, must be done at once, as there is no time to be lost. I therefore respectfully suggest that as you will receive this letter early tomorrow morning you should come up to town immediately on receipt of it, and meet me. I will be waiting at the principal bookstall at Paddington Railway Station at six o'clock sharp tomorrow evening, when I shall expect the honor of seeing you. It will be well, however, to send me a telegram as soon as you get this, addressed to me at Spring Street P.O., London, W., saying if you are coming or not. I may remark that delay will be dangerous, as the matter must be attended to at once."

Jennison who had carefully cut off the heading of the hotel note-paper, and had provided himself with a plain envelope addressed this epistle unsigned to Lady Cheale, at Cheale Court, Chester, and took it himself to the branch post office close by the hotel. He there ascertained that it would be delivered by the first post next morning, and then dropped it into the box with something of the feeling enjoyed by a gambler who flings down a master card. And shortly before noon next day, calling at that same post office, he was handed a telegram, the message part of which contained but one word: Coming.

Chapter 9

Jennison chuckled to himself when he read the one word of that telegram. He felt pretty much as a spider might feel if it saw a fat and succulent fly walking deliberately into its parlor. He crushed the flimsy paper in his hand as he went out of the post office, and in the street tore it into a thousand sheets and dropped them in the gutter as he walked along; instinct prompted him to do this as a precautionary act of the highest importance. It wouldn't be well, he argued, if anything happened to him, a street accident or something of that sort, to be found in possession of letter or message from Lady Cheale. But Lady Cheale! Ah, Lady Cheale knew a damn sight more, sir, about that Alfred Jakyn business than she'd let out, so far...no error about that! And Lady Cheale was frightened...frightened of him, Albert Jennison! He had her in a leash...he could pull her this way and that, wherever and whenever he liked. He felt very grateful to the far-away President of the Western Lands Development, or whatever they called the thing, for offering five thousand pounds for news of Alfred Jakyn: he wished that worthy gentleman had gone a step farther and made it ten thousand. For whatever the amount, he felt sure he could get it and a bit over from Lady Cheale. Lady Cheale had a reason for keeping out of the business, and she'd pay...through the nose. He meant to let her see plainly when he met her that evening that she'd just got to pay and that the market had improved. Six thousand would be a fair price now...what was worth five thousand to those American johnnies was worth six thousand to Lady Cheale.

Ruminating over what he considered the biggest stroke of luck he had ever known in his hitherto uneventful existence, Jennison strolled along to the corner of Praed Street. It was not yet noon; he hadn't to meet Lady Cheale until six in the evening, and he began to wonder what to do with himself: leisure was unusual to him. But chancing to glance across the street he saw, alighting from a motor omnibus at the other side, the young gentleman who, as a pushing reporter, had interviewed him after the first inquest proceedings, and whom he remembered by the name of Trusford. Trusford, alert as ever, was standing on the pavement by this time, staring about him as if uncertain of his whereabouts. And at that, Jennison, resolving to keep an open countenance and close thoughts, crossed over and hailed him. Trusford started, grinned, and held out a friendly hand.

"Hallo, old bean!" he exclaimed. "What're you doing in these parts and in your go-to-meeting raiment? Where's the City?"

"Hang the City!" said Jennison. "Left it...come into a bit of money. What're you doing round here?"

"Lucky devil!" remarked Trusford. "Don't go through it too quickly, though. What am I doing round here? Same game, my son! Haven't you seen my stuff in our holy rag every morning? I've been set apart, detailed, told off, to lay all my talents to work on that Jakyn case...making quite a feature of it, we are. Of course, a lot of the stuff I've written up so far is tripe...mere theory, suggestion, that sort of thing. But it keeps the public...our public...on the hop, and by-and-by I guess I'll hit something big...may be going to within the half hour, possibly."

"How?" asked Jennison.

Trusford pointed across the road.

"Come over to that saloon-bar and do a drink, and I'll tell you," he answered. "Don't mind telling you, as you're in the affair, so to speak. You don't know anything more yourself, I suppose, anything new...?"

"No!" replied Jennison. "Haven't been in the way to hear anything...been down in the country most of the time since I saw you."

"Well, all this is between ourselves," said Trusford. "Keep it dark! I'm only telling you because you promised to post me in anything you got to hear of, as, of course, you will, eh?"

"Oh, of course!" agreed Jennison. "You're welcome to any news I get."

"Well, this of mine may be something good and again it mayn't," said Trusford, leading the way into the saloon bar and up to its counter. "What's yours...bitter beer? Best stuff, too, this time o' day. Well, bring your liquor into that corner, and I'll show you a bit of English as she's wrote."

Jennison looked on with close attention and absorbed interest while Trusford produced from a capacious pocket, evidently crammed full of papers, an envelope fashioned of extremely common, whitey-brown paper, and drew from it a leaf obviously torn from a cheap account book.

"This," said Trusford, assuring himself by a glance that they were out of earshot in their corner, "was delivered at our office, addressed to the name of the paper only, and was in due course handed to me. There's illiteracy all over it...big! but it may mean something. Read it!"

Jennison took the dirty, much creased leaf, and read:

"Dere Sur, If so be as the man wot writes them pieces in your paper about the Cartright Gardins affare likes to call at Petharford Mews, nere Paddington Stashun, and ask eny of the men wot he sees about for Shino, I can tell him sumthink wot may have toddo with wot he calls the mistry, though not sure, but likely to be worth knowing of and thort I would akwaint your paper with the same your truly is same should call between twelve and one o'clock noon if my most convenient me been then there for my dinner as a rule."

"What d'you think of that?" asked Trusford. "Queer name, Shino, isn't it?"

"Nick-name, I should imagine," said Jennison. His wits were already at work, and he was wondering how to turn this to his own advantage. "Why should this chap apply to you instead of to the police?" he asked.

Trusford laughed the laugh of superior knowledge.

"Ah, my son!" he answered. "You don't know these fellows as I do. That order has the greatest objection to telling anything to the police. But they'll tell a newspaper man. Perhaps they think the police should find out things for themselves; perhaps there's a natural enmity between 'em. Anyway, newspapers can get hold of information that the police never touch. Of course, I'm going to see Shino, whoever he may be. Now, where is Petherford Mews? You know?"

"No...but any policeman will," said Jennison. "There's one at the corner."

"And we won't ask him," remarked Trusford. "We, too,

can do without the police. We'll ask a taxi-man...there's a rank over there. Most of these mews have been converted into garages, though they retain their names."

Petherford Mews, duly discovered, and within a hundred yards of where they had been talking, proved to be precisely what Trusford had prophesied. Instead of horses and vehicles, the mews was now full of taxi-cabs and their drivers, and one of these, to whom Trusford made application on entering the yard, nodded an instant affirmative to his question.

"Shino?" he said. "That's him...a-getting his dinner there...that's Shino!"

He pointed to a fat, red-faced man who sat on an upturned box ten yards away industriously consuming cold meat and bread with the aid of a large clasp-knife. Seen at close quarters, he appeared to be wrapped up in several overcoats, two or three mufflers, and a pair of knee-boots; above the mufflers a pair of small, shrewd eyes looked out above weather-beaten cheeks. Those eyes examined the two young men closely as they drew near, and fixed themselves finally on Trusford.

"Your name Shino?" asked the reporter.

"It ain't, gov'nor, and that's a fact!" answered the man readily. "But it's the name I'm known by, and what I wrote to you in...for I reckon you're the newspaper chap as I was expecting?"

"Just so!" agreed Trusford. "Came to see you at once, of course."

Shino pointed his clasp-knife at Jennison.

"And this here young toff?" he asked. "Who's he? 'Cause I ain't going to have nothing to say to no blooming detective, nor plain-clothes man neither!"

"Oh, that's all right!" answered Trusford, reassuringly. "He's nothing of that sort...he's a friend of mine. I'll answer for him. You can say anything you like before him."

"Ain't going to say nothing at all, guv'nor, till I knows if it's going to be worth something," declared Shino. "And as I've been a-studying of it and think it is, I want to know how you're a-going to line my pocket. You newspapers pays well for news...so I'm told."

"You can depend on me," replied Trusford. "If what you

have to tell is really good stuff, you'll get a nice reward. Look here! I'll give you a fiver now, for whatever it is, and if it turns out to be valuable, you shall have more. What do you say to that?"

He drew a five-pound note from his pocket and handed it over, and Shino, securing it with avidity, shut up and put away his clasp-knife, and rose to his feet.

"I says that'll do very handsome, guv'nor, and I trusts you for the balance!" he exclaimed. "But I ain't going to talk in this here yard. You come along o' me to a quiet little place as I knows on, just round the corner, and I'll tell you all about it over a pint of ale."

Jennison was becoming used to hole-and-corner work, and he felt quite at home when the man who had news to sell conducted him and Trusford to a snug resort in an adjacent street, where, reinforced by a pint of beer and a pipe of strong tobacco, he gave signs of knowing all about it.

"Leastways, approaching thereto, guv'nor!" said Shino. "Me having read your paper constant, and being a bloke as can put things together, I'll tell you honest what I know, and to show what they call boner fydes I'll give you my proper name and address, which it's Clarence Augustus Johnson, Beamer Street Flats, Clerkenwell, and well known to everybody round that way as a highly respectable man what's never been in no trouble. Clarence Augustus—but you can call me Shino...it don't hurt none!"

"Well, what do you know, Shino?" inquired Trusford.

"This here, guv'nor! Of course, I used to drive a hansom in the old days, but since all this here motoring come in, I've took to taxi-cab business. I works the big stations, as a rule...Euston, St. Pancras, King's Cross, and I works late of a night a good deal. Now, on that there Monday night when the bloke fell down and died in Cartwright Gardens, I was going towards Euston station, when, at, as near as I can tell, twenty minutes to eleven o'clock, two men...gentlemen...stopped me at the corner of Charles Street and Seymour Street..."

"Where's that exactly?" asked Trusford.

"Just off the Euston Road, guv'nor...north side. They asked me if I was engaged, and when I said I wasn't, they told me to take 'em up as far as the Cobden Statue..."

"Where's that, too?" demanded the reporter.

"Corner of Eversholt Street...which is a countinywation of Seymour Street and Hampstead Road, guv'nor. They got in, and I took them there."

"Short ride?" asked Trusford.

"Matter o' half-a-mile, guv'nor. They gets out at the statue, and one of 'em gives me half-a-dollar. 'Look here,' he says, 'you wait here, just where you are. But if we aren't back in twenty minutes, you can go.' Then they walks off...sharp, as if they was in a hurry."

"Any particular direction, Shino?"

"That's what I'm coming to, guv'nor. Yes...they goes down Crowndale Road. And I lights my bit o' baccy and waits."

"Did they come back within the twenty minutes?"

"They did, guv'nor. They comes back within the time...a minute or so within the time. In they gets again, and tells me to go back to where I picked 'em up. I does so. They gets out there...corner o' Charles Street and the man what had give me the first half-dollar gives me another. They parted as soon as they got out o' my cab...one, him what give me the half-dollars, goes along Charles Street; t'other, he walks forward towards the Euston Road."

"And that was the last you saw of them, Shino?"

"The very last, guv'nor. I been round that quarter many a time since, o' nights...of course, it's my beat...but I ain't seen neither on 'em."

"What makes you think this has something to do with the Cartwright Gardens affair?"

"Well, guv'nor, I read your paper careful about that business...every piece what come out in it. And I see the picture of the man what died, mysterious-like, in Cartwright Gardens...Jakyn. Seemed to me that I saw a likeness between that there picture and one of the two men I been telling you about."

"Which man?"

"Not the man that did the talking, guv'nor...t'other. Him what walked away to the Euston Road when they parted. Of course, it was a dark night, and them streets in that quarter isn't over well lighted, but I see both men pretty plain, and it did strike me as there was a resemblance when I see the picture in the paper to the second man...him what didn't do no talking. He was a tallish, fair-complexioned chap, that, and he hadn't no overcoat on...he was in a dark suit, blue serge, as near as I can hit it."

"Sounds like Jakyn," murmured Trusford. "He was fair-complexioned, and he had a dark blue serge suit. But the other man, Shino...what was he like?"

"I see more of him...noticed him more, like...as he did the talking," replied Shino. "He was a taller chap than t'other, dressed all in black...big black overcoat and one o' them big black slouch hats. But I see little of his face, 'cause he was wearing a white muffler about his neck and half his physog was buried in it. What bit I could see of his face he seemed to be one o' the pale-face sort."

"Did you see where the two men went when they turned down Crowndale Road?" asked Trusford.

"I didn't, guv'nor...I gave it no attention. My opinion is that they turned down a side street...there's two or three about there. Wherever they went they weren't long away, so they couldn't have gone far."

That was all that Shino could tell, and Trusford, bidding him keep his knowledge to himself and promising further reward, left him and went away with Jennison.

"That's Jakyn we've just heard about!" he said, when they were out in the street. "Jakyn, as sure as fate! But...who was the other man? And where did they go in Crowndale Road? And why?"

"I suppose you'll print all this tomorrow?" suggested Jennison.

"Do you, my son?" laughed Trusford satirically. "Then we shan't! I shall keep every scrap of that to myself until I know more. You keep it dark, too. Look here! if you're doing nothing tomorrow, drop in at our office, and we'll have another talk...you might help me about looking round that Euston district."

Jennison promised, indifferent in reality as to whether he would keep his promise or not. He had added to his stock of knowledge, but he had no intention of adding to Trusford's. Just then he had his own work to attend to and at six o'clock it led him into Paddington station, to look out for Lady Cheale.

Chapter 10

Between leaving Trusford and keeping his appointment, Jennison did a lot of serious thinking. He had little doubt that the second of the two men seen by Shino on the night of Alfred Jakyn's death was Alfred Jakyn himself. Jennison, in consequence of many years' residence in it, knew the Euston district of London as intimately as he knew the one street of his native village. And when he left the newspaper reporter and went off to lunch at his hotel, he reckoned up times and distances, bearing the taxi-driver's story steadily in mind. It was a bit like a jig-saw puzzle, thought Jennison, but a very, very easy one! Everything pieced together splendidly, and everything fitted in and round Alfred Jakyn.

Just before ten o'clock Alfred Jakyn leaves the Euston Hotel, and at ten meets Lady Cheale at the west end of Endsleigh Gardens. He and Lady Cheale turn into the saloon of the Cat and Bagpipe, close by. They leave it about ten-thirty: from then a veil falls over their movements. Or...had done so, until Shino lifts it. Supposing Shino's man in the dark blue serge suit is Alfred Jakyn, then things come out quite clearly again. It would take Alfred Jakyn, an alert, vigorous man, eight or ten minutes at the very outside to walk from the Cat and Bagpipe to Charles Street. Take it for granted that he did walk to Charles Street, Lady Cheale having parted with him outside the tavern, and returned to her hotel...what was obvious then, was that he went, hurried, perhaps, to Charles Street, to meet another person.

That person, undoubtedly, was the man in the black clothes and white muffler. With him Alfred Jakyn at once repaired to the corner of Charles Street and encountered Shino and his cab. The times again fitted in perfectly. When Shino brought the two men back and set them down, and Alfred Jakyn walked away, it would be, almost to a second, exactly ten minutes past eleven. And from that point in Cartwright

Gardens where Alfred Jakyn collapsed and died, it was...at the rate he was walking when Jennison saw him from his open window...only a few minutes' walk. So he had ample time to do it...too much time, indeed. And Jennison settled over his coffee and cigarette that there were three points arising out of what Shino had told:

1. Who was the man who got into the taxi-cab with Alfred Jakyn?

2. Why did this man and Alfred Jakyn go to Crowndale Road?

3. Did Alfred Jakyn call anywhere or meet anybody during the time which elapsed between his leaving Shino's cab and falling dead in Cartwright Gardens?

And after that came another, which, Jennison being constituted as he was, interested him far more than the previous three: How far did all this concern him in his dealings with Lady Cheale? In other words, how was he going to profit by his chance meeting with Trusford, the reporter, and Shino, the taxi-cab driver? He had no illusions now as to his own policy. Perhaps, he said to himself, he had first gone into this thing from a desire for change, a longing for adventure, but from an early stage of its progress he had seen that there was money, big money, in it, and thenceforward his one idea was personal profit. And as he had said, earlier in the day, chuckling over the welcome thought, the market had improved: that American cablegram had altered things. With the knowledge that what he could tell was worth some or all of five thousand pounds to the signatories of that message, he could approach Lady Cheale with more confidence. Lady Cheale, for reasons of her own, wanted her name suppressed, wanted to be kept out of it...at all costs! And therefore...Lady Cheale would pay.

He began to wonder, as he lounged away his time in the hotel smoking-room, if Lady Cheale knew anything, anything really definite, about Alfred Jakyn's movements after they parted company with him outside the Cat and Bagpipe? Did she send him to that Charles Street district? Did she suggest his going there? It was certainly significant that within a comparatively short time of his leaving her he was in the company of a man in Charles Street, who, taking the times into consideration, must have been waiting for him. Did Lady

Cheale know that man? Did she know why he and Alfred Jakyn went together to Crowndale Road? Questions...all questions, mused Jennison: it was wonderful, and puzzling, too, how one question was generated by a previous one. And when he began to speculate on yet one more...would it be wise in his own interests to tell Lady Cheale what he had learned from Shino, and watch the effect on her? It would show her that he, Jennison, knew more than she was aware of; that he was in earnest, was seriously at work, and might suddenly hit on a discovery that would ruin her. Should he lay his cards on the table and let her see that...

But he dismissed the idea as speedily as it had arisen. No! he would keep to his policy of saying as little as possible, and learning all that he could. He was absolutely sure of one thing...Lady Cheale would do anything, pay anything, to keep secret the fact that she met Alfred Jakyn and was with him in the saloon of the Cat and Bagpipe for half an hour on the evening of his death. That was good enough for the present state of affairs; a strong string on which to play for a time; he would stick to it until he saw reason to try another. And if he could get any news out of Lady Cheale, any information, any hint or suggestion, all the better.

Lady Cheale came to the place of meeting appointed by Jennison at the exact moment he had fixed. She was plainly dressed, and heavily veiled; it was obvious to Jennison, watching her from a carefully-selected point of observation, that she did not wish to be recognized or to attract attention. And Jennison, having made sure, as far as he could, that she was unattended, went quietly up to her and greeted her in his politest fashion...politeness, he was well aware, cost nothing. But this politeness produced no more than a mere nod from Lady Cheale...a silent intimation that she was aware of his presence. Yet he saw that for all her reserve of manner she was nervous, and he was clever enough to avoid letting her see that he saw anything. He drew away from the crowd around the bookstall, signifying by a glance that she should follow and in spite of her chilly attitude, she followed.

"Where do you want me to go?" she demanded in a low voice. "I'm not going..."

"Nowhere where you don't wish to go, Lady Cheale," interrupted Jennison.

"There's no need! We can do our bit of talk anywhere...walking up and down this platform, if you like. But I should suggest a cozy corner in the tea-room...why not be comfortable while we're about it?"

She made no opposition to that, and Jennison led her into the tea-room, found a quiet nook, and took upon himself to order tea. And when the waitress had left them he looked across the table and smiled...confident in his own powers. But Lady Cheale gave him a glance which would have made a more observant man remember that if you corner a cat it will probably fly at you.

"This is all right, I think," said Jennison.

"Why have you brought me to London?" demanded Lady Cheale suddenly.

"Obvious!" retorted Jennison. "Circumstances have changed since I saw you. By the announcement in the paper...which I sent you and which, no doubt, surprised you!"

"No!" answered Lady Cheale. "I wasn't surprised."

"Not?" exclaimed Jennison, taken aback. "Not by that...that offer from the American people? Why not?"

"Because I expected something of the sort. He...Alfred Jakyn...told me he was over here on business for that company. I thought they would offer some reward for news of him."

Jennison remained silent for a minute or two, drumming the table and staring at her. He hadn't expected this; it put a new complexion on things. And before he could think what to say, Lady Cheale spoke again.

"It's no affair of mine that they have offered a reward," she said. "All I am concerned with is that it should not be known...for reasons of my own...that I saw and was with Alfred Jakyn that evening, between ten and ten-thirty. I paid you to keep silence on that point, and bought that note from you. Without that note you can prove nothing..."

"Oh, but you're wrong there!" said Jennison, hastily. "The note's nothing! There's the evidence of the girl...the barmaid..."

"I should deny it," interrupted Lady Cheale calmly. "My word is as good as hers: better, indeed. I should say she was mistaken...I wasn't there. I repeat...now that the note is destroyed, you can't prove that I met Alfred Jakyn."

The waitress came with the tea just then, and her presence for a minute or two gave Jennison a chance to think over his next move. He resolved on a bold one.

"Lady Cheale," he said, bending across the table when they were once more alone, "just understand, once for all, that you're wrong! I didn't tell you everything when we were talking in your park last Sunday afternoon. The truth is, I know a lot more than you've any idea of. Now, you say you were with Alfred Jakyn from ten to ten-thirty on the evening of his death, and you imply that you know no more of his movements. Very good...let me tell you straight out, I don't believe you! For, though I haven't told you up to now, I know of his movements after ten-thirty! And to prove to you that I do, let me mention the names of two streets in the Euston district to you...Charles Street, Crowndale Road! Now, Lady Cheale, how does that bit of news strike you and what do these names suggest? Come!"

He saw at once that his stray shot had gone home. Lady Cheale turned pale, and an undeniable look of fear came into her eyes.

"What...what do you know about those streets and...and Alfred Jakyn?" she asked. "What?"

Jennison shook his head.

"Enough to warrant me in going to the police and claiming that reward!" he answered. "Come, Lady Cheale, let's do business! I don't want to go to the police...I want to keep my bargain with you. But you must see that the market's improved...since last Sunday. That American offer has sent up my stock by leaps and bounds, Lady Cheale! It's like this...I can go and sell my information to these people for five thousand pounds. Therefore, it's worth five thousand pounds...to you!"

He was watching her closely, and he saw a certain sullen look come over her face.

"You're blackmailing me," she muttered. "If I told the police..."

"You know as well as I do that you're not in a position to tell the police anything, Lady Cheale," said Jennison quickly. "If you go to the police at all, they'll ask awkward questions. They'll want to know a lot about your doings that evening, and about your relations with Alfred Jakyn: they'll want..."

"I'm not concerned with what they'd want," said Lady Cheale. "What do you want?"

"Not to lose anything!" replied Jennison promptly. "I want as good terms from you as I could get from these American people. I've got the knowledge, the information...I'd far rather sell to you than to them. Or, to put it plainly, I'd far rather you paid me not to sell to them. Come, now!"

Lady Cheale, who had made but a mere pretense of drinking her tea, suddenly picked up her handbag and rose.

"Meet me here tomorrow morning at half-past twelve," she said. "Be in here...you can order some lunch or something. That's all I'm going to say now...but I shall be here alone, at the time I've mentioned."

She went swiftly away between the tables, and for half a minute Jennison remained in his place watching her go. Then a sudden notion shot into his mind, and, slipping some silver into the hand of the waitress with a hurried whisper that he couldn't wait for the change, he hurried after his late companion. The sudden notion was that he would follow her. For he had an idea that Lady Cheale was probably going to consult somebody as to her further action in this matter, and if she was, he wanted to know where she went and to whom.

Jennison had no great trouble in tracing his quarry along the crowded platform. At that hour of the early evening Paddington station was densely thronged by folk going homeward to western suburbs and up-river resorts, and he found it easy to keep himself unseen while he kept Lady Cheale in sight. His one fear was that she might get into a taxi-cab and drive away before he could hail another. But instead of turning to the entrance of the station she went straight down the long departure platform to the sloping subway leading to the Underground Railway. He followed her down that, moving still more warily lest she should turn and see him. But the subway was even more crowded than the station above, and it was easy work to follow her along there and through the barrier on to the Metropolitan and District platform. That, too, was thronged, and Jennison saw at once that as long as he kept himself at a safe distance he could keep an eye on Lady Cheale's movements with ease and safety.

An east-bound train rattled in, and Lady Cheale slipped into a first-class car. Jennison entered the next, placing himself in such a position that he could watch the exit of the other. He foresaw that his chief difficulty would be when Lady

Cheale got out of the train; the farther east they went, the fewer passengers would leave; people did not go to the City nor to the East End at that hour; rather, it was just then that everybody came away from those quarters, at the end of the day's work. He would have to be cautious when Lady Cheale and he left that train, he said to himself...one glance behind, on a stairway, or in a passage, and she would see him. But fortunately for Jennison's plans, Lady Cheale left the train at Euston Square, where, luckily, a great many other passengers left it to catch trains in the big terminus close by, and within a couple of minutes Jennison found himself in the familiar Euston Road, with Lady Cheale, all unsuspecting and unconscious of his presence, a dozen yards ahead of him.

Jennison now began to think that he was wasting his time and his ingenuity, and that he had followed Lady Cheale merely to see her go into the Euston Hotel, where, he knew, she usually stayed when in town. But he was speedily reassured; instead of making for the Euston Hotel, Lady Cheale turned away and went up Seymour Street. And she had not gone far up there when she turned again...into Charles Street...and Jennison suddenly realized that he was probably on the verge of the biggest discovery he had yet made. For it was of Seymour Street and Charles Street that Shino had talked that morning and here they were, and here was Lady Cheale, pacing their frowzy pavements, and here was he, Jennison, dogging her footsteps!

It was a poor, shabby, down-at-heel and out-at-elbow district that, smelling of all sorts of nasty things from cheap burning oil to fried fish, and Jennison wondered whatever had brought Lady Cheale into it. But presently Lady Cheale disappeared. She shot aside, swiftly, into a doorway; the doorway of a shop or office, the lower part of the one window of which was obscured by white paint, on which were two lines of black lettering. Using as much caution as a cat, Jennison stole up to the place and read the lettering as he slipped past. What he read amazed him as much as the fact of Lady Cheale's having gone in there.

SURGERY
Hours, 6.30 to 9.30 p.m.
Advice and Medicine, Sixpence.

As soon as Jennison saw that, he shot across the street...to reflect and to watch. He had heard of these cheap places before; places where you got medical advice and a bottle of stuff for half a crown or a shilling, but he had never heard of a six penny establishment. Yet there it was and Lady Cheale was in it. Very well...

Jennison watched from across the street for some time. He saw several poorly-clad people enter and leave the surgery door. At last he crossed over, and, after inspecting the window, found a place where the paint was worn off, and peeping through it, looked into the interior. He saw a sort of waiting-room, shabby and ill-furnished, and just then empty; at its farther side was a door, wide open, communicating with an inner room. And in that he saw Lady Cheale talking, rapidly and earnestly, to a man who wore a white linen coat, and he had his back to Jennison. But suddenly the man turned, and Jennison knew him at once. Dr. Syphax!

Without pausing to consider or reflect, Jennison stepped to the outer door, pushed it open, and walked in upon Lady Cheale and her companion.

Chapter 11

Had Jennison been less absorbed in his own affairs he would have remembered, long before he stepped into the Sixpenny Surgery, that the American cablegram, addressed by its sender to Scotland Yard, and reprinted in every newspaper in London, and by many in the provinces, must needs have been read, and with avid interest, by several hundreds of thousands of people. He might have reflected, too, that out of that vast mass of readers, some few, at any rate, had, or fancied they had, a chance of establishing a claim to the reward of five thousand pounds. But he had no such remembrance, nor any such reflection: a born egoist, he went on his own way, never pausing to speculate on what somebody else might be doing. And thus absorbed, he completely forgot Miss Chrissie Walker.

But Chrissie had not forgotten Jennison, nor their conversation, nor its subject. Not a devourer of newspapers at any time, she took a sort of duty look at the organ supplied to the Cat and Bagpipe every morning; she had to know a bit about the day's news, she opined, in order to be able to talk to customers. And in common with the hundreds of thousands of folk above-mentioned, she saw the announcement of the President of the Western Lands, and at once realized that, unlike most of her fellow-readers, she had something to tell. It was not much, no doubt, but it was something, and it was...definite. She had seen Alfred Jakyn on the evening of his mysterious death. She could point to the very seat in which he had sat in the saloon bar of the Cat and Bagpipe.

She could testify as to his companions. She was prepared to identify that companion. She could swear...positively...to the hour at which Alfred Jakyn walked into the Cat and Bagpipe, and the hour at which he walked out. All that, in her opinion, was something. But...was it worth anything? She determined to ask Jennison about that; Jennison, she believed, was a smart young fellow, a clever young fellow, who could write real poetry. And he was in the City…where all the brains are. Of course! Jennison would know. But Jennison did not come to the Cat and Bagpipe. As a rule, he showed up there pretty nearly every night: came and sat on a stool at the bar, drank his bitter beer, smoked his pipe, chatted…all friendly-like. He had not been for some days, however, when Chrissie read the tempting announcement, and he did not come that day, nor the next.

Perhaps he was ill; perhaps he was away on business; anyway, she was not going to wait for ever. And at noon on the third day, when a youthful customer, whom she knew to be a junior clerk in a solicitor's office close by, came in for a mouthful of bread and cheese and a half-pint of ale, Chrissie, alone in the bar with him, began to fish for information.

"You wouldn't charge me anything, George, would you, for a bit of advice?" she asked, leaning confidentially across the counter. "You wouldn't be sending me a long bill, with six and eight pence at the bottom?"

"No fear, old thing!" responded George, graciously. "Anything that I can do…free gratis, to you. And what might it be, now? Not a case of breach of promise, I hope? Impossible!…in your case, old thing."

"I ain't even engaged," replied Chrissie. "No hurry to be, either, thank you. No! it's this. Supposing, now, you happened to know something…not much, you know, George, but just a little thing…that you knew the police were very anxious to know, what would you do? Supposing, of course, it was you?"

"Um!" replied George, composing his features to the semblance of wisdom. "What should I do if I knew something that I knew the police wanted to know? Um! Just so! Well, I think I should proceed with caution! Like this, for instance. I should first consider what would be the result if I told the police. You wouldn't like to give a friend away, old thing!"

"Oh, it wouldn't be giving a friend away," declared Chrissie. "I wouldn't think of such a thing, of course. Oh, no, nothing like that! Just telling the police a mere…well, a mere fact."

"In that case, I should tell 'em," said George. "In fact, as a…er, as a member of the community…I could put it in legal parlance, only you wouldn't understand it…you're bound to assist the police by any and every means in your power. If you know something that relates to what we'll call the administration of justice, you're bound to declare it. Public service, old thing!"

"Then would you tell the first policeman you see?" asked Chrissie.

"Decidedly not, old thing!" exclaimed George. "I should go to headquarters, to a responsible official, or to the nearest police station. Secret communication, old thing! private and confidential you know."

"That's what I want...private and confidential," said Chrissie musingly. "They wouldn't tell, then?"

"Anything of a strictly confidential nature would be regarded as...as strictly confidential," replied George. "Of course, if you want your confidence respected, there's nothing like coming to one of us legal practitioners. You wouldn't like to confide in me, old thing?"

But Chrissie thought not: it was one of those things, she said, that wanted thinking about; nevertheless, if she required more advice, she'd certainly apply to George for it.

"Couldn't come to a better man, old thing!" said George. "Of course, if it's beyond my power...I don't say that it is, nor that it isn't...but if it's a point of law, we can fix you up at our shop, and I'll see you ain't charged, either...leave it to me. But one point, old thing...in all matters connected with law and police, bear this in mind...go slow! Count twenty! Take the advice of an old stagger...a month's reflection is better than a day's haste!"

Chrissie, however, had no mind to reflect for a month, nor for a day. She had two hours' liberty every afternoon, and on the very day on which she asked George's advice, she set forth from the Cat and Bagpipe in her best bib-and-tucker, and went round to the nearest police station, which happened to be that whereat Womersley, the detective, was temporarily engaged, and to which the unraveling of the Cartwright Gardens mystery had been originally consigned. And there she soon found herself closeted with a uniformed official who, being well acquainted with all the taverns of the neighborhood, recognized her as soon as she walked in.

"And what can we do for you, Miss Chrissie?" he inquired good-humoredly. "You haven't come to give yourself up, eh?"

Chrissie treated her interrogator, whom she knew well enough by sight, to a confidential smile.

"It's about that Cartwright Gardens affair, Mr. Brown," she answered. "There's a piece in this paper about it...a reward. Five thousand pounds! And..."

"Good Lord! do you know anything about it?" exclaimed the police official, genuinely surprised. He took the paper from his visitor's hand, and glanced at the announcement. "Yes," he continued. "I saw that. But...do you know anything?"

"I know something," replied Chrissie. "It's like this, Mr. Brown. I saw Alfred Jakyn the evening that he dropped dead in Cartwright Gardens!"

"You did?" said Mr. Brown. "Where? When?"

"At our place...the Cat and Bagpipe," answered Chrissie. She went on to tell what she had already told Jennison, and the official listened intently. "I could identify the lady, if I saw her again," she concluded. "I took her all in! She...was...a lady, and in evening dress, too."

Mr. Brown considered matters. Here, at any rate, was information entirely new to the police. And he was so busy in speculating on its probable worth that he forgot to ask his visitor a highly important question...if she had already told this news to any other person?

"I wish Womersley had been in," he remarked. "He's the detective that's at work on this Alfred Jakyn case. But I'll tell you what...he'll be back here about six o'clock, and I'll send him round to you. You'll be in?"

"I go on duty at six o'clock," replied Chrissie. "It's always pretty quiet up to seven...tell him to come round as soon after six as he can."

Mr. Brown promised that Womersley should be at the Cat and Bagpipe by half-past six at the latest, and after a little more conversation he saw Miss Walker to the door of the police station, and watched her go away up the street. It was then a quarter to five o'clock in the afternoon and from that moment Miss Walker completely disappeared. Womersley walked into the police station at six o'clock, and Brown told him of the barmaid's visit and her information.

"She's absolutely positive about the man being Alfred Jakyn," said Brown. "And she'd evidently taken close stock of him and his companion. So..."

"Why the deuce couldn't she have come round long since?" interrupted Womersley irascibly. "She must have known this ever since she saw that paragraph in the newspapers, and that's days ago! Days wasted! There's been some reason why she didn't come...somebody's persuaded her to keep quiet."

Brown shook his head.

"She said nothing of that," he remarked. "And I don't think anybody has. My idea is that she's just...waited."

"Waited for...what?" sneered Womersley. "Till the spirit moved her? And if it's that reward she's after...as no doubt it is...why didn't she come three days ago, when the announcement first appeared? There's something in this that she hasn't told...she's got some confidant, or something of that sort, and probably came here as a feeler."

"Oh, well!" said Brown, puzzled by Womersley's suspicions. "I suppose you'll step round there and see her?"

"Oh, I'll step round," assented the detective. "Somewhere close to Endsleigh Gardens, isn't it? Hang it! if she'd only come at once, as soon as she saw that photograph, one might have made some use of her information about Jakyn's companion! Now...all this time lost!"

He went out grumbling, and grumbled all the way to the Cat and Bagpipe. For Womersley, so far, had had no luck in this Cartwright Gardens affair, and he was vexed with everything connected with it, and with himself. He could make nothing of this job. Nobody could tell him anything fresh. He had talked to Bradmore and come away no wiser. He had interviewed Miss Belyna Jakyn and got nothing out of her.

He had gone to the length of waylaying Dr. Syphax's one domestic servant, for the purpose of ascertaining from her that Belyna spoke the truth when she said that no other members of the family than herself were in the house when Alfred Jakyn called there. He had traced men with whom Alfred Jakyn had traveled from New York to Liverpool; he had worked out his movements from Liverpool to the Euston Hotel. Nothing had come of all this; not the ghost of a clue. And he was particularly vexed with the Home Office experts; they gave him no help. They said that Alfred Jakyn had been poisoned...but they did not know, and weren't certain, that they ever could know by what particular poison.

They were strongly of the impression...belief, if he liked...that the poison had been administered about an hour before death took place, but weren't certain about that; there were limits, sarcastically remarked one of them, to even their knowledge of toxicology. And Womersley wasn't getting on at all, and his professional spirit was affronted; he had ambition, and wished to rise, and here was just the sort of case he had always wanted, and he was up against a blank wall.

"If this confounded barmaid had only come to me at once," he growled as he turned into the side street wherein stood the Cat and Bagpipe, "I might have traced that woman! But with all this time gone..."

He walked into the saloon bar, and found it empty; there was no one behind the counter, and no customers in the cheery, comfortable room. But at the sound of Womersley's entrance, a man's face showed itself at an inner door...a man who had discarded his coat and turned up the cuffs of his smart white linen shirt, and who, from his general attire and air of prosperity, the detective took to be the landlord.

"Evening, sir!" said this individual. "What can I do for you, sir?"

Womersley went up to the counter.

"Have you a Miss Walker here?" he asked bluntly. "Miss Chrissie Walker?"

The man behind the counter pulled a face.

"We have, sir...er, as I should say, we had!" he answered. "And why I say had is that she ought to be on duty now, and isn't, as you can see, which is a confounded awkward thing for me, for I'm short-handed in the other parts of the house, and got my misses poorly in bed, too. Miss Walker went out this afternoon, for her usual time off, and she's never come back! Ought to ha' been in by six, at the latest...but no sign of her. You're wanting her? Anything I can do?"

Womersley pulled out his professional card, and laid it on the counter. But the landlord nodded before glancing at it.

"Oh, I know you, Mr. Womersley!" he said. "I've seen you a time or two. You've forgotten me, no doubt, but I was on the jury at that inquest on Alfred Jakyn."

Womersley had been considering where he had seen the landlord before; now he remembered, and with an air of confidence he drew a stool up to the bar and perched himself on it. "To be sure!" he exclaimed. "I thought I knew your face. Well, it's about that very case that I want to see Miss Walker. She called at the police station this afternoon when I was out, and told Brown, who was in charge there, that she knew something about the Jakyn affair. So I came round to hear what she's got to tell...though, as a matter of fact, she told Brown."

"Good heavens, you don't mean to say that!" exclaimed the landlord. "She? Why, what on earth does she know about it? Never said a word to me, on my life. What did she tell Brown?"

Womersley repeated what Brown had told him; the landlord listened open-mouthed, and full of astonishment. But at the end he nodded.

"Ah!" he said. "Um! That may explain something. Do you remember a young fellow who gave evidence at that inquest...Jennison?"

"Of course!" said Womersley. "That's the chap who saw Jakyn collapse in Cartwright Gardens. He lives there...he saw Jakyn out of his window."

"Just so," agreed the landlord. "Well, now that I'm reminded of it, I saw Jennison in here one night...of a week or so ago...talking to Miss Walker, confidential-like. He's a regular customer here...of an evening...so I thought nothing of it. But now...I wonder if she told him about this?"

Womersley thought it uncommonly likely, but kept his thought to himself. He waited a little while to see if Miss Walker came in, but as she had not returned at the end of half an hour, he went away, telling the landlord that he'd look in later in the evening. Once outside he walked straight to Cartwright Gardens and there, at the scene of Alfred Jakyn's mysterious death, knocked at the door of the house in which Jennison had lodged. And as he waited for some response, he thought about Jennison. Somehow, he had always had a suspicion about that young gentleman...a suspicion that Jennison had not told all that he might have told. He remembered now that Jennison had been very keen about going with him to see Bradmore, that he had poked his nose in amongst the newspaper reporters, that...

The door opened...a few inches. A half-grown, slatternly, down-at-heel girl, a typical London lower-class lodging-house looked out on him. No, the misses wasn't in; she was out. Mr. Jennison? Oh, no, he wasn't in either, he didn't live there now; he'd gone away. No, she didn't know where he'd gone, but he'd took all his things with him.

Womersley went back to the Cat and Bagpipe. He was certain by that time that the barmaid had told Jennison what she knew about Alfred Jakyn. But what did Jennison know? And had he told her what he knew? If she had returned...

But when Womersley looked into the saloon bar for the second time, the landlord shook his head. Miss Chrissie Walker had vanished...from his ken, at any rate.

Chapter 12

"Not a sign, nor a sound!" said the landlord. "Ain't so much as showed her nose at the door! Queer! I can't make it out, I can't! If there was any reason..."

He paused, looking at his visitor with an air of helpfulness, mingled with a sort of wonder, as if he had an idea in his mind that Womersley might know something. But Womersley was wanting information.

"You don't know of anything?" he asked.

"Nothing!" said the landlord. "Nothing!"

"Money all right?" inquired Womersley, with a significant glance at the cash register.

"Oh, yes!" exclaimed the landlord. "Nothing of that sort, my boy! Perfectly honest young woman...been with me six months...no complaints of any sort to make against her...none!"

"Any love affairs?" asked Womersley. "Elopement...eh?"

"None as I know of," said the landlord. "Very straight, nice girl...friendly, chatty, and so on with the boys, but hadn't any particular one, I believe. No! can't think of any reason why she should go off like this. She always seemed well satisfied, here."

"London girl?" inquired the detective.

"She was not!" replied the landlord. "No...he came to me from Buckinghamshire; Aylesbury. People live there, I fancy. But of course we can find out."

"If she doesn't come in tonight," said Womersley, "you'd better go through anything she's left behind...letters, and that sort of thing and see if you can find any address you could write to. I'll look round in the morning."

He was going off with no more than a nod, but the landlord called him back. "Half a minute!" said the landlord. He gave Womersley a keen, knowing look. "What's your opinion of it, now?" he asked confidentially. "Do you think, now, between ourselves, it's anything to do with her going round to the police station? Because...well, there it is! She goes there, tells one of your people something and disappears...clean! Queer, I call it! Now, what do you think?"

"Can't say!" replied Womersley curtly. "Nothing to go on...yet. As I said just now I'll look in tomorrow, early."

But it was with no expectation of hearing anything definite that he returned to the Cat and Bagpipe next morning, and he felt no surprise and made no comment when the landlord told him that Miss Chrissie Walker was still missing. The landlord wanted to discuss things more thoroughly, with a view to action, but Womersley bade him wait. Womersley felt that Jennison had something to do with the barmaid's disappearance; if he could only get hold of Jennison, he said to himself, he would soon get hold of the girl. And once more he went round to Cartwright Gardens, and this time Jennison's old landlady was in, and quite ready to talk. She poured out all that Jennison had told her when he left.

"Come into money, going to get married, and live in the country, was he?" said Womersley. "And who was he going to marry, and where was he going to live?...did he tell you?"

"Which he did not!" answered the landlady. "He was all in a hurry, like. You see, he'd been away for some days, and he came back sudden, and took me all unawares, and just told me what I've told you, and away he went again. And, of course, I haven't seen him since."

"Do you know where he was employed?" asked Womersley.

The landlady knew, and gave him the address of the City warehouse which Jennison had left so unceremoniously. And Womersley took himself, and saw the manager, and presently discovered that Jennison had told one tale in the City and another in Cartwright Gardens, and his suspicions deepened and his detective instinct began to awake.

"Oh! come into money and was going to travel on the Continent, was he?" he remarked. "Um! I suppose you haven't seen him since...you, or any of your clerks?"

The manager replied that he'd neither seen Jennison, nor heard of him since he left the firm's employ. He went to inquire if any of Jennison's old associates had news of him, and presently came back with a strange-looking youth, who eyed Womersley with curiosity.

"Nobody's seen him since he left here," reported the manager, "but this young man says he knows something about him that he thought a bit strange at the time."

Womersley turned on the young clerk; the young clerk grinned knowingly.

"Well?" said Womersley. "What do you know?"

"You're a detective, aren't you?" asked the young clerk. "Just so!...I saw your name in connection with that Jakyn case, in which Jennison gave evidence. You found a draft, or a check, or something of that sort, among Jakyn's effects when you examined them at the Euston Hotel, didn't you?"

"Well?" assented Womersley, alert to new possibilities. "And what of it?"

"It was on the Equitable Trust of New York...London Branch, in King William Street, wasn't it?" continued the clerk. "Just so. Well, a few days after the inquest, I saw Jennison coming out of the Equitable Trust in King William Street. That was during lunch-time...I was having a stroll round there."

Womersley, in spite of his training and his natural reserve, could scarcely repress a start of astonishment on hearing this.

"You did," he exclaimed. "Then...did you speak to him? Did you ask him what he was doing there?"

"I didn't do either," replied the clerk. "He seemed to be in a hurry...shot off as soon as he came out. And...well, I wasn't on sufficiently friendly terms with Jennison to ask him questions of...of a private nature. Only, I thought it rather an odd thing that he should have been to the very bank that was mentioned in your evidence."

Womersley thought so, too, and he went away from the warehouse wondering what Jennison had been up to...everything pointed to some underhand business on Jennison's part. He went round to the Equitable Trust office in King William Street and made inquiry. Yes, Jennison had certainly been there...to ask if they could give him any information about Alfred Jakyn. That must have been the very day after the opening of the inquest on Alfred Jakyn. They had no information to give him and he hadn't been back since.

Womersley left the bank wondering why Jennison had ever gone there at all. But he was by this time absolutely certain that Jennison was playing some queer and deep game in connection with the Cartwright Gardens affair. The thought nettled him. He had viewed Jennison, at first, as a bit of a fool. He had humored him by allowing him to accompany him to Bradmore's, believing that Jennison was just wanting to satisfy an idle, perhaps morbid curiosity. But he now felt that behind Jennison's surface simplicity or stupidity there was a good deal of cunning, and that, either from the very beginning, or from some early point of this business, he had been playing a game of his own. And...what game?

Had he told everything he knew, at the opening of the inquest? Had he told the truth about the actual facts of Alfred Jakyn's collapse and death? Was he shielding anybody? Was there any one he could implicate, if he liked? Was somebody paying him to keep out of the way? It looked like that...Jennison had thrown up his job, left his old lodgings, told people that he'd come into money; said to one that he was going to travel, to another that he was going to get married. What was his game? and who was in it, besides himself?

All this speculation led Womersley to go into the Alfred Jakyn case again from the beginning, and he spent a couple of hours that day in reading and re-reading the evidence given before the Coroner, the information, fragmentary enough, gathered since, and his own memorandum, which were few and inconclusive of anything. And in the end, he determined to start out on the whole thing once more, and to begin with he set off to see and re-question the smoking-room waiter at the Euston Hotel; he wanted to question him, with more attention to detail, about Alfred Jakyn's movements just before he left the hotel on the evening of his death.

But Womersley was met by another tale of sudden and inexplicable disappearance. This particular waiter, a youth of nineteen or twenty, had never come to his work the previous evening, and had never been seen at the hotel since. According to the man whom Womersley saw, he should have come to his duties at half-past five, but he neither came, nor sent any excuse for his absence. Now, in the ordinary course of things, Womersley would have thought nothing of this...the lad might have been indisposed, and had no one by whom he could send a message. But when he remembered that the barmaid of the Cat and Bagpipe had mysteriously disappeared in the same neighborhood, on the same day, and at about the same time, he became more suspicious than ever, and felt certain that the two disappearances, in some queer way, were related to each other.

"Do you know where this lad lives?" he asked his informant. "I've a particular reason for wanting to see him, at once."

"Oh, I can tell you that!" replied the man. "He lives at a sort of club, up Camden Town, where a lot of young fellows of his sort live...residential club, they call it. Two or three of our waiters live there...cheaper than lodgings, they say, and better accommodation."

Womersley took the precise address, and going off to the place, got hold of the club steward. And within a couple of minutes he knew that he was up against another mystery, as strange and unexplainable as that of the barmaid. For the man he wanted was not there, and had not been there the previous night nor at any time during the present day.

"I don't know anything about him, nor where he is," said the steward. "I saw him go out of here last evening, at his usual time, and I've never seen him since. He never came in last night...that I'm certain of."

"Did he look as though he was going to his work at the hotel when he went out?" asked Womersley.

"Oh, yes! He'd his waiter's clothes on...dress coat, white tie, and all that," assented the steward. "He was a smart chap...particular about his get-up...always looked very spic and span. Yes, he just went out, as usual."

"What was his time for coming in?" asked Womersley.

"Quarter to twelve," said the steward. "I know he never came in last night, because I wanted to see him about his trying to get a job for a young friend of mine, and I looked out for him. He's certainly not been in here since he went out." Then he gave Womersley an inquiring look. "What's the trouble?" he asked. "Is he in any?"

Womersley told the man enough to satisfy him, and went away, wondering. His methodical, matter-of-fact mind began to tabulate things; he visualized them as if they were set down before him in a schedule:

1. Jennison, who had lodged at one house for several years, and worked for the same time at one warehouse, suddenly

forsakes his lodgings and gives up his job, and vanishes.

2. Chrissie Walker, whom Jennison knew, goes to the police station and gives certain information, and walks out and disappears.

3. The young waiter at the Euston Hotel sets out to his work at his usual time, and between his residential club and the hotel is lost to all knowledge as completely as Chrissie Walker and Jennison.

And underneath that bald statement of fact, Womersley saw one word...Why? Why? Yes, it was nothing but why! why all the time! Why had Jennison made himself scarce? Why had Chrissie Walker, who ought to have been behind her bar at the Cat and Bagpipe at six o'clock last evening, disappeared as completely as if she had been snatched into the clouds? Why had the young waiter in his eight or ten minutes' walk between the residential club and the Euston Hotel vanished as thoroughly as if the earth had opened and swallowed him? And...had all these three disappearances a connecting link? They must have...there must be a thread running through them, and the devil of it was that Womersley, at that moment, hadn't the remotest idea of how to put a finger on either end of it. He went back, moody and dissatisfied, to the police station, intending to have a chat with his officials there before going home for the day. But as he walked in a man at the door stopped him.

"There's a gentleman waiting for you, Mr. Womersley," he said. "Been here half an hour on the chance of your coming back. There's his card there in the rack...he's in the little room, back of the office."

Womersley was so full of his own affairs that he took up the card with little interest; certainly there was no speculation in his mind as to its presenter and his business there. But one glance at it showed him that the man who was awaiting him had come, and come a long way, in the hope of solving the mystery that was puzzling him, and he hurried along the drab, dismal corridor with something of excitement, murmuring his visitor's name...Mr. Edward Holaday.

"This is the chap they said they were sending over," he reflected. "Wonder what he's like? Typical cute Yankee, no doubt, who'll think we're all half asleep on this side. However..."

He pushed open the door of the little room and advanced into it with an inquiring look that changed to a stare of something like astonishment at what he saw. For Mr. Edward Holaday seen at close quarters was not at all like anything in Womersley's own line of business, nor would Womersley, coming across him in the street, have ever taken him for a man likely to solve criminal problems or prove mysteries. He was a tall, loosely-built, big-boned young fellow of apparently twenty-eight or thirty years of age, whose garments, not at all English in cut, were evidently worn with more regard to use and comfort than to style and fashion, whose boots, very prominent at the toes, were of colossal size, and whose general aspect was more that of a countryman from a long way back than of one accustomed to town life. This impression was deepened by Mr. Holaday's umbrella, which was of unusual dimensions, and might have been copied from that once owned by Mrs. Gamp, and further by the fact that the collar of his flannel shirt was tied up by a bootlace. As for the rest of him, he had a smooth, clean-shaven face, a pair of ingenuous blue eyes, and a smiling mouth; his expression, indeed, was almost cherubic, and it was only when he stretched out a hand which closed round Womersley's in a steel-like grip that the detective realized that this odd-looking customer was a fellow of immense physical strength.

"Mr. Womersley?" said the visitor heartily. "Glad to see you, sir. I called in at your headquarters as soon as I struck London this afternoon, and they told me I'd find you at this branch station so I came right along. You would know, Mr. Womersley, that our people of the Western Lands were sending me here about this Alfred Jakyn case? you'd be expecting me?"

"Yes," assented Womersley. "Yes." He was a bit taken aback, a bit uncertain. He motioned his caller to sit down again, and sat down himself. "You're not fully acquainted with all the facts, I suppose?" he went on. "As you've only just arrived..."

"Just so, but I cabled to an agent of ours to collect all the newspaper reports for me," interrupted Holaday, with an ingenuous smile. "And," pointing to a pile of papers at his elbow. "I have them here and have already gone through them...hastily."

Womersley hesitated a moment before he spoke again. He was still studying his visitor. And he was quick enough to see that Holaday, on his part, was studying him.

"Well!" he said at last. "I may as well tell you, Mr. Holaday, that I don't think Alfred Jakyn's murder sprang out of anything relative to his connection with your company. That's my opinion...at present."

Holaday smiled...why on earth, wondered Womersley, was his smile so extraordinarily like that of an easily pleased child? and tapped his pile of papers.

"That may be so, Mr. Womersley," he said. "And...it mayn't. But I'd like to tell you at once that whether it's so or not, I'm here to solve, or to assist in solving, the mystery of Alfred Jakyn's death! That's what I'm out for and I guess I'll just go along...preferably with your kind assistance...till I get there!"

"Got any idea?" asked Womersley, half-chaffingly. "I suppose you have!"

Holaday nodded and this time there was no smile.

"Well!" he answered, slowly. "I may as well tell you...I have!"

Chapter 13

The detective gave his visitor a long and steady look; Holaday replied to it with one just as steady and as long. And at the end of this mutual inspection, the American rapped out a word...staccato fashion.

"Fact!" he said.

Womersley got up, glancing round the drab little room with an air of distaste. He pointed to Holaday's pile of newspapers.

"Come out and have a cup of tea with me," he said. "Bring those...we'll have a quiet talk about this affair. There's a decent restaurant close by...we'll be comfortable there."

Holaday unwound his long length from his chair and rose...he was lanky enough, thought Womersley, when he stood up; he himself felt a midget beside him. Outside, in the half-fog of a chilly evening, he glanced at his companion with some secret amusement.

"Ever been in London before, Mr. Holaday?" he asked.

"No...nor in England, until a few hours ago," replied Holaday. "Furst time!"

"How's it strike you?" inquired Womersley, laughing.

"Just that things are pretty close together," said Holaday. "I was no sooner out of Southampton than I was in London. There's an advantage in that, too."

He said this so gravely that Womersley laughed again.

"Yes, we're pretty tightly compressed," he remarked. "Still, there's a lot of waste ground here and there." He turned into a restaurant at the corner of the street and led his companion to an alcove near an open fire. "That's better!" he said, rubbing his hands. "We can talk in peace and comfort here. And there's a matter I want to know about straight off, if you'll tell me," he went on when he had summoned a waitress and given her his order, "and it's this...what was the secret mission that Alfred Jakyn came across about? For when I examined his belongings at the Euston Hotel I found no particulars of any mission...no papers, you understand, no business papers. Not a line!"

Holaday smiled in his ingenuous fashion.

"You wouldn't," he said. "He had none. His mission was here," he continued, tapping his forehead. "He didn't need any papers. He came here, Mr. Womersley, commissioned to see some big men...capitalists...to whom there was no necessity to show papers or documents; all his business was to be done by word of mouth."

"Then, in that case, why do your people think that he was got rid of because of his business?" asked Womersley. "I took that to mean that he'd something on him, or in his possession, which somebody wanted to get hold of. Wasn't that it?"

"No!" replied Holaday. "That's not at all our notion. Our notion, Mr. Womersley, is that he was just got rid of, put out of action, before he could even begin his business. We think it possible that Alfred Jakyn was followed across."

"Well," said Womersley slowly, "I don't know. I've made a lot of inquiry about his movements and so on during the voyage, and I've seen and talked to men who came over with him, and to a couple of well-known London business men who traveled with him from Liverpool to London, and I haven't hit on anything that contributes to that theory. You think there are people to whom his business in London wouldn't be welcome?"

"There are people across there, Mr. Womersley, to whom Alfred Jakyn's business in London on behalf of our company would be very unwelcome," said Holaday. "And some of them are people who wouldn't stop at anything in their anxious time to render it impossible for him to even start on that business. Of course, until we got the news from London that Alfred Jakyn was dead, we were of the firm belief that not a soul in the world knew on what business he'd gone over, and it may be that even now nobody did know. But when you come to consider the circumstances, you can easily understand our position."

"I suppose Jakyn was fully trusted by you?" asked Womersley. "You'd every confidence in him?"

"Alfred Jakyn, Mr. Womersley, had been in the employ of our company for close upon nine years," replied Holaday.

"He'd been chiefly in pretty far-off places, and had had some stiff jobs to tackle and ticklish negotiations to carry out. He was a very trusted servant, and a clever man...but even the cleverest man is vulnerable, and can be taken in by a cleverer man than himself."

"There's no doubt that Alfred Jakyn was poisoned and in a damned clever fashion, by a proficient!" remarked Womersley. "Got any theories on that?"

"Oh, piles or I had," answered Holaday. "He might have had a drink with an enemy, all unsuspecting, on leaving the boat at Liverpool, or on parting at Euston...oh, yes, I've theorized considerably on those points. But I'm putting that aside...I want now, with your help, to start clean out afresh, right from the moment, as it were, when Alfred Jakyn collapses in that street and dies. I've read all this," he went on, tapping his bundle. "Hastily, of course, but still, pretty thoroughly, and I got these papers on landing at Liverpool this morning...they were awaiting my arrival...I read them in the train. So I know the facts...main facts, right up to date. Now I'd like you to tell me...is there anything new that I don't know?"

Womersley considered this question in silence for a minute or two. But he was taking a liking to his queer-looking companion, and presently he spoke frankly.

"Well, yes, there is," he answered. "Some rather strange things have come to light since yesterday evening. I was puzzling my head about them when I met you just now. It's like this," he continued, "three people have disappeared mysteriously within the last twenty-four hours, all of whom had a more or less close connection with the Jakyn case. But I'll tell you the details." He went on to set out, in order, all the facts relating to Chrissie Walker, to Albert Jennison, and to the young waiter, from the time of the barmaid's visit to the police station to that of his own inquiries at the residential club. "What do you make of that?" he asked in conclusion. "Come!"

"Why, that it all centres round the woman who went with Alfred Jakyn into the oddly-named tavern!" replied Holaday, with a laugh. "We'll have, of course, to find out who that woman was. That surely ought not to be such a difficult thing. Trace her...that's the business."

"There are between seven or eight millions of people in this place!" remarked Womersley grimly. "And a considerable proportion of that crowd's women. I haven't the ghost of a clue to this particular one, now that the barmaid's vanished."

"Find the barmaid...I'll help," said Holaday cheerfully. "But, well, as to women...now you asked me, away in that police station, if I'd an idea, and I said I had. It's not an idea as to who murdered Alfred Jakyn, or anything of that sort; it's not a cut-and-dried theory. It's just an idea that came to me in reading the various accounts in these newspapers; an idea that I feel sure should be followed up...investigated to the full, and at once. And...it's about a woman."

"A woman?" exclaimed Womersley. "What woman? I don't remember any woman in the case, except Jakyn's aunt, Mrs. Nicholas Jakyn, and his cousin, Miss Belyna, and I've gone into particulars about both, and convinced myself that Miss Belyna gave truthful evidence, and that her mother wasn't in the house at Brunswick Square when Alfred Jakyn called there. What woman do you refer to?"

Holaday, while Womersley was talking, had been balancing a teaspoon on the edge of his cup, smiling quietly either at his efforts to establish its equilibrium or at something in his mind. He now replaced it in his saucer, and turning to his companion, dropped his voice and asked an unexpected question. "That's all very good, but say!...who was Millie Clover?"

Womersley slewed round in his seat in sheer surprise at the American's question. For the life of him he could not remember the name which Holaday had pronounced with peculiar emphasis and significance. He sat knitting his brows and racking his brains for a full minute, while his companion watched him, evidently wondering at the effect of his question.

"That's it!" said Holaday. "Millie Clover! Who was or is...Millie Clover? Seems to me a mighty important feature, that!"

"I don't remember any Millie Clover," answered Womersley.

"No?" exclaimed Holaday. "The girl Alfred Jakyn asked about at Bradmore's...the chemist?"

"Oh, that!" said Womersley. His tone was almost contemptuously indifferent.

"Pooh! That was a mere question about some girl or other who'd once worked in the chemist's shop...typewriting girl, or something...long since. Nothing in that!"

But Womersley shook his head.

"Look at here," he said earnestly. "I guess there may be a lot in that! You put it to yourself, now. Alfred Jakyn comes back to England after some ten years' absence. He goes to his father's old place of business and finds that his father's dead, and that the former manager, Mr. Bradmore, has taken on the whole concern. Alfred Jakyn...I'm going on the accounts given, mind...talks to Bradmore about various things; hears about his father's intestacy, and his aunt and his cousins, and such-like. But of all the people he'd known in the old days, he only asks about one...Millie Clover. Why does he ask about Millie Clover, unless...eh?"

"Well," asked Womersley, reluctant to confess that he didn't follow, "why does he...in your opinion?"

"Why, because, after all these years, he's still interested in her," replied Holaday. "I reckon that! Why? There must have been lots of people he could have inquired about, but he doesn't...he only asks after Millie Clover. And I guess he wanted to see Millie Clover."

"Bradmore didn't know anything about Millie Clover...as far as I remember," remarked Womersley.

"Quite so...but that doesn't prove anything against my idea," said Holaday. "And Alfred Jakyn may have found out Millie Clover's address after leaving Bradmore. I reckon he could turn up directories and so on."

"Not much time or chance that night," objected Womersley. "His time's fully accounted for."

"No!" said Holaday. "I think not. Supposing he was at this queer-named inn, or tavern, or whatever you call it, with the mysterious woman, until half past ten o'clock, there's still an hour and a quarter to account for."

Womersley nodded his agreement: evidently, he said to himself, this chap was no fool.

"Well," he asked, "what do you want to do?"

"As I said at the beginning, I'd like to start out from what I feel to be the initial stages," replied Holaday. "I'd like to see Bradmore, the chemist."

"That's easy," said Womersley. "We can stroll along there now if you like...it isn't ten minutes' walk. By the bye," he continued, as they left the restaurant, "where are you staying?

Have you got a hotel?"

"Oh, I'm staying at the Euston, where Alfred Jakyn put up," answered Holaday. "I went there because I wanted to be right on the spot. That's a pretty handy hotel, I reckon, and expensive, but my instructions are to spare neither time nor expense in solving this mystery...especially expense. I've a free hand in the money line."

"And supposing you find that Alfred Jakyn's murder, if it was murder, had nothing whatever to do with your company?" inquired Womersley. "What then?"

"It'll be a vast relief to us," said Holaday, gravely. "No news would be more welcome to our president and our management! We're sorry enough to lose an active and valuable man like Alfred Jakyn, but nothing would give us such satisfaction as to be fully convinced that his murder sprang out of some cause with which we've nothing to do."

"The fact is," observed Womersley dryly, "you want to be certain that your secret, whatever it is, has neither leaked out nor been endangered. Eh?"

"Well, sure!" admitted Holaday. "I guess that is so."

"All right!" said Womersley. "Let's walk down to Bradmore's."

Bradmore stood behind his counter in the Holborn shop. He was making up a prescription, and as he held up a bottle to the light, staring at its contents abstractedly, he looked to Womersley more melancholy than ever. He nodded to the detective in silence, and seemed but faintly interested when Womersley introduced his companion as Mr. Holaday of New York.

"We want a few words with you, in private, Mr. Bradmore," said the detective. "If quite convenient, of course."

Bradmore finished the compounding of his mixture, fixed a cork in the bottle, stuck a label on the bottle's side, and methodically wrapped it up before showing any sign that he had heard what Womersley said. Then he called to a youth who was rolling pills in the background, and bidding him attend to the counter, motioned his visitors to follow him into a parlor at the rear of the shop. There he pointed to chairs, and taking one himself, nodded at the detective in token that he was listening. And Womersley, knowing something of his man by that time, went straight to the point.

"Mr. Bradmore, this gentleman has come across from New York to inquire into this mystery about Alfred Jakyn," he said. "He's discussed all the known facts with me, and he's anxious to get an answer to a question. There's no other person I know of who can give that answer but you. The question is...who was Millie Clover?"

The two callers were watching Bradmore intently, but one more than the other, and it seemed to him that the chemist started. But his voice was composed enough when he spoke.

"She was correspondence clerk, shorthand writer, typist, in this shop in the time of my predecessor, Daniel Jakyn," he said. "She was here...perhaps eighteen months. That's eleven years ago...eleven years, I mean, since she left."

"You knew her?" suggested Womersley.

Bradmore gave him a queer look in which there seemed to be a sort of pitying amusement.

"I've been here as apprentice, assistant, manager, proprietor, thirty years!" he answered. "Of course, I knew her!"

"And Alfred Jakyn knew her, too, I suppose?" asked Womersley.

"Oh, yes, he knew her. Everybody connected with the business knew her."

He looked from Womersley to his companion, as if asking what he wanted, and Holaday spoke.

"Alfred Jakyn inquired about this girl, Millie Clover, when he came to see you?" he said quietly. "Made particular inquiry, I understand, Mr. Bradmore?"

"Well, particular in the sense that she was the only person he did inquire about," answered the chemist. "He wanted to know if I knew anything about her, and where she was to be found. I knew nothing and told him so."

"Did he say why he wanted that information?" asked Holaday.

"He didn't. He just asked that and when I answered him, as I've told you, he said no more."

"You know nothing whatever about Millie Clover, then?" suggested the American.

"Nothing...now. I've never seen nor heard of her since she left this business, more than eleven years ago. She left suddenly...for what reason, I don't know."

Womersley got up. He began to button his overcoat in

sign of departure.

"Blank wall!" he muttered. "I didn't think Mr. Bradmore could tell us anything."

But Holaday was sitting still.

"Oh, but I guess Mr. Bradmore can tell us lots...yet!" he said, with one of his ingenuous smiles. "I'm not going to bother him to-night, though, except on one little matter. Mr. Bradmore, I've no doubt you could tell me, perhaps by taking a little trouble, where this Miss Millie Clover lived when she was employed here."

"Eleven years ago!" exclaimed Womersley. "Ages...in London!"

Holaday smiled again, looking at the chemist. And suddenly Bradmore nodded.

"Yes," he answered. "I could do that, I believe. I have all the old books and papers belonging to the business stored at my house, and I can look them over at the dates I've referred to. I dare say the address is there...sure to be, I think. Where are you staying? Very well...if I find the address I'll drop you a line by the midnight post."

Outside the shop, Holaday gave Womersley's arm a squeeze.

"Good business!" he said, with a chuckle. "I shall get that address!"

"What good will it be?" asked Womersley. "Eleven years ago! as I said before."

"Come round to my hotel early in the morning," said the American. "Then...maybe I'll tell you...if I've got a line from Bradmore."

The line from Bradmore awaited his rising next morning. It was literally a line, penciled on a half sheet of paper and enclosed in an envelope. He chuckled again as he read it.

c/o Mrs. Shepstall, 93a St. Mary's Square, W.

Chapter 14

Womersley walked in upon Holaday as the American sat at breakfast in a quiet corner of the hotel coffee-room: Holaday, with a cheery nod, held up the slip of paper.

"Got it!" he said. "That's step number two! Worth while going to see the chemist man, wasn't it, now?"

Womersley dropped into a chair and glanced at the address.

"What do you expect to make of this?" he asked, half cynically, half jokingly. "It's merely the address of the woman with whom the girl lodged. That's eleven years ago! The woman's probably dead, or she's left...it's big odds against your finding her. And if you do find her, what do you imagine she'll know of this girl, whom, no doubt, she hasn't seen, nor heard of, for many a year? London landladies don't take much interest in lodgers who come and go."

Holaday helped himself to another cup of coffee and sipped it with an air of reflection. But it seemed to Womersley that he was not reflecting on Womersley's remarks.

"This St. Mary's Square, now," he said presently. "Where is it? and how long will it take to get there?"

"It's in the Paddington district," replied Womersley, "and it would take a few minutes on the Underground."

"Well, isn't it worth a few minutes to go there and inquire if this Mrs. Shepstall still lives at this address, and if she does, to ask her if she knows anything about Miss Millie Clover?" said Holaday. "I guess it is! We're not economizing on time to that extent."

"Oh, well, if you're bent on it, I'll go with you," agreed Womersley. "But I'd like to know what it is that makes you so keen on this Millie Clover business? What's your notion?"

"My notion is that Alfred Jakyn himself was keen about getting news of Millie Clover," replied Holaday. "Why did he inquire about her at Bradmore's if he wasn't? He didn't inquire about anybody else. There must have been lots of old friends he could have inquired about. But he didn't! He just asked for news of Millie Clover. Well, I want to know why!"

Womersley shook his head. He was beginning to think that Holaday, in spite of a shrewdness already made manifest, had something womanish about him, that he trusted to intuition.

"Can't see it even now," he said, with a sceptical smile. "I attached no importance to his having asked for news of Millie Clover, when I first heard that he had. I put the thing this way...there he was, back in the old spot, and naturally he asked after people associated with it. His father was dead; Bradmore was there before him; this Millie Clover was the only other person he remembered. And...perhaps he was a bit sweet on her in the old days."

Holaday threw back his head and laughed, joyously.

"I thought you'd get round to it in the end!" he said. "Now that, of course, is just the notion that's been in my mind all along! That's precisely why he did ask for news of her. I reckon that he wanted to find her. And as I said last night, we don't know that he didn't contrive to get some news of her that evening he called at Bradmore's. Now I propose to get on the track of Millie Clover, and if I find her and I will, if she's alive and in this country! to ask her what she knows about Alfred Jakyn, last as well as first. And I hope you'll go right along with me to see this Mrs. Shepstall."

"Oh, I'll go with you!" answered Womersley. "As you say, a few minutes is neither here nor there: I can spare them. By the bye, I've had no further news as regards the three disappearances I mentioned to you yesterday. The barmaid affair puzzles me most...nothing has been heard of her."

"I think they all run into one another," said Holaday. "And they all center in, or spring from, the incident of the Cat and Bagpipe, the woman incident. Now, look here...has it occurred to you that the woman who went with Alfred Jakyn into that saloon, and sat there talking with him for half an hour, may have been this very Millie Clover that I'm so keen on tracing?"

"Good Lord, no!" exclaimed Womersley. "I'd certainly never thought that! Seems a far-fetched notion, but..."

"Well, it's what I call a highly probable thing," said

Holaday, "and it won't surprise me any if it turns out that the woman was Millie Clover. And if it was so, then I think you'll find that there's probably been a pretty weighty reason for these disappearances. Well...I'm through with this breakfast, and if you'll show the way to this St. Mary's Square..."

The small houses on the north side of St. Mary's Square looked dull, drab, and dismal enough in the foggy November morning. Holaday shivered, involuntarily, at the sight of them.

"Lodging-houses, I reckon?" he said. "And I suppose this Mrs. Shepstall, if she's still alive, and still here, will be what they call in the books a typical London landlady, though I haven't the ghost of an idea what the type's like! Sort of women who've seen better days, I guess?"

"Most of 'em say so," answered Womersley. "Not much difference between them and any other woman, I think. For my purposes and I've had to interview a good many of 'em in my time...they're divided into two classes; the women who'll talk and the women who won't. Some of 'em take you into their best parlors at once, and pour out a flood: some, metaphorically, keep their door on the chain, and show you no more than a nose-end. But here's the place. Now, if this woman's existent, will you do the talking, or shall I?"

"Say, I think you'd better tackle that," replied Holaday. "You know your customer better than I do. I'll listen and observe."

"Well, I'll lay you two drinks to nothing that we don't find Mrs. Shepstall," said Womersley, as he tapped the knocker. "She'll be gone! Eleven years in London is as good as a century elsewhere."

But Mrs. Shepstall was there. She opened the door herself; an elderly, quiet-mannered little woman, who sized up the quality and probable business of her visitors as soon as she saw them, and without question or hesitation led them into a sitting-room just within the narrow hall. Womersley handed her his professional card.

"You see who I am, Mrs. Shepstall," he said. "This gentleman is an inquiry agent...Mr. Holaday, from New York. We're investigating a case which has many difficulties, and we believe you may be able to give us some information. Now, can you tell us anything of a Miss Millie Clover, who, we're given to understand, lodged with you in this house, some eleven or twelve years ago?"

Mrs. Shepstall immediately nodded, and motioned her visitors to sit down.

"Oh, yes!" she answered. "I can tell you something about her. Miss Clover lodged here for some fifteen months or so...she had this very parlor as a sitting-room...about the time you mention. She was in business..."

"Yes, at Daniel Jakyn's, chemist, in Holborn," said Womersley. "That's where we got your address."

"Yes, it was at Jakyn's," assented Mrs. Shepstall. "She was a clerk and typist there. A very nice, pretty, well-conducted young lady, very superior in every way: I was sorry when she left me. She went suddenly, too...very suddenly. To get married."

"Oh, to get married, ma'am?" said Womersley. "Then I suppose you know who the gentleman was?"

But Mrs. Shepstall shook her head.

"No," she answered, "I don't! never did; it all came on me as a surprise. I knew nothing about it; hadn't the faintest idea that she was going to be married. She called me in here one morning after breakfast, and told me she was getting married that day, and shouldn't be coming back. She'd a small suit-case already packed; two trunks that she had, in her bedroom, she asked me to take care of until she sent for them. And then, after settling my bill, and giving me something for my maid, she was off...all before I'd time to ask her who she was marrying, and where the wedding was to be, as I certainly should have done if she hadn't been in such a hurry."

"Then I suppose she left Jakyn's in the same hurry?" suggested Womersley. "You don't know about that, of course, ma'am?"

"I don't know for a certainty," replied Mrs. Shepstall. "But it was on a Monday morning that she left me, and, of course, she might have finished at Jakyn's on the Saturday. It was a complete surprise to me, the whole thing, for I didn't know she was engaged. Nobody...I mean any young gentlemen...ever came here to see her, and I never knew her have anybody bring her home. She was certainly out a good deal of an evening, but I never knew that she had any young men friends...she didn't seem that sort."

Womersley nodded, and then turned to Holaday with a

look which seemed to imply that for the moment he could think of nothing else to ask. But the American, who during this colloquy had been silently nursing his queer umbrella and watching Mrs. Shepstall attentively, let out two words.

"The trunks?"

Mrs. Shepstall looked at him with an understanding smile. "Oh, yes!" she said. "Of course, there were the trunks. I thought she'd come and fetch them...I knew she'd got a lot of good clothes in them...she was rather a dressy young lady. But she didn't come and didn't come...for years. Indeed, she never did come!"

"Then you have them?" asked Holaday.

"No!" replied Mrs. Shepstall. "I haven't. It would be about seven, perhaps eight years after she'd left that I got a letter from her asking me if I'd send the trunks to the address from which the letter was written, and of course I did. I can show you the letter, if you like."

"We should like, ma'am," said Womersley. "There's nothing we should like more. It may be most useful."

The landlady left the room, and the two men glanced at each other.

"Well," said Holaday, in his driest manner, "I reckon we're not wasting our time!"

"I wonder who she married?" remarked Womersley, musingly. "Odd! That Mrs. Shepstall never knew she'd a young man."

"The young man may have been as sudden an event as the departure," suggested Holaday. "And it mayn't have been a young man, either."

"Well, a man, then," agreed Womersley. "Of course, the marriage could be traced."

"Easily?" inquired Holaday.

"Oh, fairly...the records are available. But we may get some information from this letter that the landlady's fetching. Seems a bit queer, you know," continued Womersley, "that she should have left these trunks here so long. It means that she must have bought a complete rig-out when she married, or have gone somewhere right away in a hurry. And why did she want her trunks after all that time...seven or eight years? The things in 'em would all be out of fashion."

"Might have come into fashion again," suggested

Holaday. "But the thing is...she did want them, and she did send for them, and gave an address, and that address, if we get it, will be another step forward."

The landlady came back with an envelope, from which she drew out a letter. She laid this on the table before the two men, and they bent eagerly over it.

"Three Shires Hotel,
"Cheltenham.

"DEAR MRS. SHEPSTALL,
"You will be surprised that I have never been to see you, nor written to you all this time, but I never really had a chance. Will you please send on to me at the above address, carriage forward, the two trunks I left with you. Trusting that you are quite well, and with kind regards.
"Yours sincerely,
"M. COLEBROOK."

"Colebrooke, eh?" said Womersley. "Her married name, I suppose. Um! there's no date on the letter."

"No, but there is on the envelope," replied Mrs. Shepstall. "There it is, you see...just about three years ago...eight years after she'd left here. I thought it strange that she should have let her trunks remain unasked for all that time, and then to have written for them in such...well...in such abrupt fashion. I sent them off, of course, at once."

"Heard anything of her since, ma'am?" inquired Womersley.

"No! she never even acknowledged the receipt of the trunks," said Mrs. Shepstall. "Not even by a postcard!"

The two men left presently, and outside the house Holaday turned on his companion with a sharp inquiry.

"Where's this Cheltenham?" he asked. "Far or near?"

"Pretty far, in this country...would be close at hand, I suppose, in yours," replied Womersley with a laugh. "It's in Gloucestershire. Famous inland watering-place...fashionable resort."

"How long would it take to get there?" demanded Holaday.

"Oh, I don't know, exactly...three hours, maybe," said Womersley. "Perhaps a bit more or might be a bit less...I've never been that way."

"Well, you'd better come, then," said Holaday dryly. "I'm going there...just now!"

Womersley came to a halt and stared at his companion.

"You don't let much grass grow under your feet!" he exclaimed. "Do you mean that? Straight off?"

"Sure! If you'll tell me what railway to take, and where the station is," answered Holaday. "I'd be a fool if I didn't! We've found out where Mrs. Colebrook, once Miss Clover, was heard of last...now I'm going to see if she's still there, and if she isn't, to trace her a bit farther. I reckon we've made what I'd call considerable progress this morning."

"Well, perhaps!" agreed Womersley. He drew a pocket time-table from his coat, and began to turn it over. "We could get an express to Cheltenham in half an hour, from Paddington," he continued. "And Paddington's only just behind those houses...that would give us time to get a mouthful to eat and a drink before starting. And I suppose..."

"Oh, come on!" exclaimed Holaday. "The next thing is this Three Shires Hotel, Cheltenham!"

And into the Three Shires Hotel, in the course of that afternoon, he led Womersley, whom by that time he had infected with some of his own enthusiasm, and who was beginning to believe, against his will, that they were really doing more good in tracing Miss Millie Clover, or, as they now believed her to be, Mrs. Colebrooke. The hotel was a pretentious one; its manager, not easily procurable, a consequential gentleman who required some assurance and guarantee of his visitors' bona fides before he was willing to talk. Womersley had to tell him a good deal before he consented to open any store of knowledge that he possessed. But when he had satisfied himself that one of his visitors was a genuine Scotland Yard man, and the other a respectable person from New York, he unbent, and having unbent, showed himself disposed to be generously communicative.

"I knew the lady you're inquiring for well enough," he said. "But you're wrong in describing her as Mrs. Colebrooke. She was Miss Colebrooke and she was my book-keeper for some little time until about a year ago, when she left to make a rare good marriage!"

Chapter 15

Womersley restrained the question that arose to his lips; he had already told the story of his and Holaday's quest, and the reasons of it, to the hotel proprietor, and it seemed to him that his best policy now was to listen and to pick up whatever information might be forthcoming. So he merely nodded, as if the announcement just made was the most natural thing in the world, one to be expected, and not to be surprised at, and the proprietor went on speaking.

"I know nothing whatever about this lady's having been known as Miss Clover," he said. "I never heard that name..she was never known by it here. She came to me as Miss Colebrooke, Miss Mildred Colebrooke, from London, where she'd been employed in similar capacities...I'd excellent references with her, most excellent. She bore them out, too...a thoroughly competent young lady, in every way; quiet, well conducted, too. Great favorite here and, as I say, she made a rare good marriage...did jolly well for herself!" he concluded, with a laugh.

Womersley let his question go then.

"Whom did she marry?" he asked quietly.

"Quite a romance!" replied the proprietor, with another laugh. "She married one of my customers, Sir John Cheale, a man old enough to be her father, though uncommonly well preserved for his age. You've heard of him, no doubt? big commercial magnate, chemicals and that sort of thing...lives at Cheale Court, near Chester. Fine place, I'm told, though I've never seen it. Sir John used to come here two or three times a year, and he took a great fancy to Miss Colebrooke, and, I believe, asked her to marry him more than once before she finally consented. However, she did consent, and she married him, and there you are! She's Lady Cheale now, wife of a millionaire or multi-millionaire...I'm sure I don't know which!"

"Have you ever seen her since the marriage?" asked Womersley.

"Well, no, I haven't," said the proprietor. "As I said, Sir John used to come here regularly, for some years, but since they were married he hasn't been. No! I've not seen her since then, of course, and it's not such a very long time since they were married."

Womersley looked at Holaday, as much as to ask if there was any question he wanted to put to the proprietor. And Holaday put one.

"Who were the people in London from whom you had references about this lady?" he inquired. "I'd just like to know that, if it's still in your memory."

"Oh, I can tell you," replied the proprietor. "I've a good memory for names. One was from a city firm, Dilwater & Crouch, of Moorgate Street, where she'd been two or three years as stenographer and typist; the other was from a medical man with a queer name, to whom she'd acted as secretary...Dr. Syphax, Brunswick Square."

It was only because he was keeping a tight hold on himself that Womersley restrained an exclamation at this news; he had begun to realize at last that he and his companion really were on the track of something, and had become watchful in consequence. Do as he would, however, he could scarcely repress a start...but the proprietor was looking at Holaday, and Holaday's face was as immobile as that of a graven image.

"Just so!" said Holaday. "And from which of these did she come to you?"

"The doctor," answered the proprietor. "He gave her a particularly good testimonial." He looked from Holaday to Womersley, from Womersley back to Holaday.

"Now, what," he asked, with a good-humoured, bantering laugh, "what are you fellows making out of all this? Are you sure that you aren't on the wrong track? From my knowledge of her, I couldn't conceive anything wrong, or suspicious, or anything of that sort, about this young lady...she's still young, you know."

"We wanted to trace Miss Millie Clover," replied Womersley. "I don't think there's any doubt that Miss Millie

Clover is identical with your Miss Mildred Colebrooke and now, it appears, Miss Colebrooke is Lady Cheale."

"Well! you'd better apply to her Ladyship," remarked the proprietor. "From my knowledge of her, she's pretty well able to look after herself!"

Womersley replied that he'd no doubt of that, and presently he and Holaday went away. They walked a little distance from the hotel in silence; Holaday spoke first, and when he spoke it was to the accompaniment of a chuckle.

"There's one great advantage of this country of yours," he said. "It doesn't take you long to get from anywhere to anywhere else! -within the boundaries. I guess we'll just get back to London and do a bit more investigation before nightfall."

"Where?" asked Womersley.

"That doctor, sure! Look here! this business is turning out more promising than I'd thought for. Things are fitting themselves. Now, last night, before going to bed, I went right through all the newspaper stuff again, more carefully, and I thought over all you'd told me...indeed, I wrote out a memorandum of that and so I'm pretty well posted in all facts and names; familiar, do you see, with the names and descriptions of the chief actors in this little play. Well now, the mention of this doctor, Syphax, by the hotel man is an eye-opener! This young woman, Millie Clover, otherwise, at one time, Mildred Colebrooke, and now Lady Cheale, was with Syphax...as Mildred Colebrooke. Well, but Syphax is Mrs. Nicholas Jakyn's brother, and so he'll have been connected, one way or another, with this Jakyn family and with that drug business in Holborn, for a good many years. He must have known Mildred Colebrooke as Millie Clover. And the thing is...what does he know about her at all, whether as Millie Clover or Mildred Colebrooke?"

"Muddling!" said Womersley, expressing his present feelings in a word.

"Well, yes, it seems a bit mixed, but I guess we'll worry through yet," replied Holaday cheerfully. "Lot of questions in it. Mrs. Shepstall says Millie Clover left her to get married. Did she get married? If she got married, she became Mrs. Somebody or other. But the next we know, keeping to a sequence, is that she was not very long afterwards employed by

Dilwater & Crouch as Miss Colebrooke; later, still as Miss Colebrooke, by Dr. Syphax. If she really did marry anybody when she left Mrs. Shepstall, where's the man? Did he die? Why did she become Miss again and not Miss Clover, but Miss Colebrooke?"

"I suppose she knows!" said Womersley. "And probably nobody else!"

"Well, I guess we'll just have to ask her to enlighten us on those points," observed Holaday in his direct manner. "That's what I intend to do...for it's my belief she knows something about this Alfred Jakyn affair, though what exactly I can't yet think. Anyway, we know where she lives, and I suggest that to-morrow morning we go down there and see her. But first...this doctor with the queer name!"

They found Syphax in his surgery that evening, busily compounding, with Belyna Jakyn similarly occupied. Syphax gave his visitors a curt reception, and did not ask them to sit down. Indeed, as soon as he saw Womersley he plumped him with a brusque question, following it up with a remark that was almost offensive in its peremptoriness.

"Well, what do you want? I know your business, and I can't help you with it! What is it? you see we're busy!"

"Not too busy, I hope, to answer a civil question or two, doctor!" replied Womersley. "I shan't keep you long. May I ask if you know anything, or knew anything, some years ago, of a young woman named Millie Clover?"

"No! Never heard of her! Who was she?"

"She was a clerk at Daniel Jakyn's shop in Holborn, eleven or twelve years ago."

"Know nothing about Daniel Jakyn's shop eleven or twelve years ago! I wasn't in England at that time."

"Well, doctor, do you know anything of a young lady named Millie Colebrooke?" asked Womersley, giving Holaday's arm a nudge.

"Mildred Colebrooke? Oh, yes...knew her well enough. She was my secretary for a time. What about her?"

"Do you know that she married Sir John Cheale, the big chemical manufacturer."

"Yes, I knew that...saw it in the Morning Post at the time. And what about that?"

"Well, we believe Mildred Colebrooke and Millie Clover

are identical," replied Womersley.

"Well, and what about that?" demanded Syphax. "And what the devil have I got to do with it?"

Womersley nudged his companion's arm again, and edged him out into the hall; behind them they heard Syphax muttering and growling.

"Come away!" whispered Womersley. "We've got what we wanted...he knew her! No use teasing him...he's a very queer, strange man! Come out! Hallo! what's this?"

A young woman, in a smart cap and apron, had come out of a door at the end of the long, dimly-lighted passage, and was making a signal to Womersley by holding a finger to her lips. As he and Holaday went towards her, she retreated to the front door and laid her hand on the latch as if to let them out into the square. But instead of raising the latch she made another warning signal.

"Is he one of your lot?" she whispered, pointing to Holaday. "With you?"

"That's right!" answered Womersley, in the same low tone. "What is it? Found anything out?" The girl looked cautiously round and stepped close to the two men.

"I can slip out in a few minutes," she said. "Meet me outside...down the square. Shan't be long."

She raised the latch as she spoke, and Womersley and Holaday walked out and turned down in the direction indicated.

"That's the girl I made some inquiries of about Alfred Jakyn's visit to that house," said Womersley when they had gone a few yards. "Parlor-maid there, smart girl...I dare say she's got a bit of information. But come! what do you think of that doctor chap?"

"Excitable, irritable person!" replied Holaday. "Full of nerves...many of them. Or lacking in them...same thing."

"Ay, but do you think he knows more than he lets out?" asked Womersley. "I think he does! You know, it's all very well going after Miss Millie Clover, and there's no doubt you were right about it being worth while, now that we've done a lot to-day towards running her down, and I don't say that something, and perhaps a good deal, won't come of it, but in my opinion the secret of Alfred Jakyn's death is in that house we've just left!"

"Sure!" said Holaday, with quiet and cheerful acquiescence. "I guess it is!"

Womersley turned on his companion in surprise.

"And how long have you thought that, pray?" he asked.

"From just about the first go-off," answered Holaday. "Good time, anyway!"

"Then why this persistence about Millie Clover?" inquired Womersley.

"My way of getting to the center-point," laughed Holaday. "There's more ways than one of getting anywhere, I reckon. Millie Clover, otherwise Mildred Colebrooke, otherwise Lady Cheale, is a detail, and I guess a mighty important one. But we'll know more about that before this time tomorrow...I think!"

"Well, maybe, if you're so persistent about it," said Womersley. "There's certainly something in it. It was no use pressing Syphax, though. By the bye, did you see that girl in his surgery?"

"I did, poor thing!" answered Holaday. "Grievous sight...mis-shapen like that. But she's a clever face and good head."

"Oh, she's clever enough!" said Womersley. "That's Miss Belyna Jakyn...Alfred's cousin; the only one of 'em who saw him when he called there. Now, you know, that girl had a chance of poisoning him...she's a qualified dispenser, and acts in that capacity to her uncle, Syphax, so I suppose she knows all about poison. And, of course, you might say she'd a motive...if Alfred Jakyn hadn't turned up, and had been presumed by leave of the Courts to be dead, she and her brother and mother would have come in for all that old Daniel Jakyn left and that, I'm told, is a rare lot of money. And I believe they come in for it now...seeing that Alfred's dead. So there's motive! But...I watched that girl carefully when she gave evidence at the opening of the inquest, and I came to the conclusion that whoever else might be guilty, she wasn't!"

"It's certain there was nobody else...none of the family...but her in the house when Alfred Jakyn called there, I suppose?" asked Holaday. "You're satisfied of that?"

"As far as one can be, yes," replied Womersley. "I've made all sorts of quiet inquiries in this case. You wouldn't believe the trouble I've taken about various small matters. I got hold of this girl...the parlor-maid...that spoke to me just now; she assured me that that night nobody was at home when Alfred Jakyn called but Miss Belyna. Dr. Syphax, she said, was often out at night...in fact, as a rule; so was Mrs. Nicholas Jakyn; so was her son, who's a medical student. None of these three, she said, were in that night until very late—well, past eleven o'clock, so...'

"The girl's coming," interrupted Holaday, looking back towards the house. "Got up in the approved mysterious fashion, too!"

The parlor-maid, cloaked and hooded, and holding her hood tightly under her chin, came swiftly towards them, and as she approached, motioned them round the corner of a quiet side street.

"I mustn't stop long," she whispered, turning to Womersley. "Now, look here; you told me that if I would get hold of any news for you, it would be worth my while. Is that going to hold good? Because, you know, I've read about that American reward..." Womersley tapped the girl's shoulder, and jerked a thumb at Holaday.

"Look here, my dear," he said, "this is the gentleman that's come to represent that firm. He'll tell you that if you can tell anything..."

"You can trust me for that!" broke in Holaday, with more eagerness than he had previously shown to Womersley. "Any information that will put us on the right track will get substantial recompense, even if it isn't absolutely final. That's certain!" The girl listened, nodded, and hesitated.

"Well," she said at last, slowly, "I don't know that what I can tell is final, but at any rate it's something, and I may get to know more. It's this...I promised him," she nodded at Womersley, "that I'd keep my eyes open, and I have done. And it's my belief that Mrs. Jakyn and Miss Belyna know something about this affair. The other day, when I was dusting the back drawing-room, I heard them talking in the front one; they came in there together, and they didn't know I was behind the curtains. They were sort of arguing, or something like that, and Miss Belyna was crying. And I heard her say something, quite plain. This, 'You ought to tell at once!' she said. 'It's sure to come out! They can't fail to find it out...especially if they get hold of Millie Clover! And they will, sooner or later; you may be sure they will! Why don't you make a clean breast of it and have done with it. I know it'll come out!'"

Womersley nudged Holaday's arm. And Holaday spoke.

"Well," he asked firmly, "and the mother—what did she say?"

"I couldn't catch what she said," replied the parlor-maid. "She spoke in such a low voice...but she seemed angry. And I was afraid of their knowing I was there, so I tiptoed out and got away. So that's all I can tell now...but..."

Womersley patted her shoulder.

"That's all right!" he said. "Now, you keep that to yourself, and go on keeping your ears open. We'll see you're right; and now run back. Well?" he continued, when the parlor-maid had flitted away into the shadows. "What do you think of that?"

"Just that I'm keener than ever on seeing Millie Clover, whose present name is Lady Cheale," answered Holaday. "So if you've that railway guide of yours handy, we'll just turn into that convenient saloon there and throw a light on its pages. And an early breakfast and the first express train to Chester in the morning will suit me admirably...the sooner we're at the door of Cheale Court the better, is my opinion!"

They were at the door of Cheale Court as a big clock in its quadrangle struck twelve next day. Holaday stared about him in surprise at the grandeur of their surroundings...but Womersley's surprise came when the door was opened by a youthful, smart-liveried footman, in whom the detective instantly recognized the vanished smoking-room waiter of the Euston Hotel.

Chapter 16

Womersley, in his time, had been a uniformed policeman, and it was in his old voice and his old manner that he fired a sharp question at the startled youth before him.

"Now then, what's this mean? what are you doing here? Come on, now!" Then, before the lad could reply, he turned to Holaday, speaking rapidly. "This is the chap I told you about, who disappeared from the Euston Hotel two nights ago...the smoking-room waiter." He whipped round on the youth again. "D'you hear, now?" he went on. "Answer my question!"

"I'm here as...as second footman, Mr. Womersley," faltered the accosted one. "I...that's why, sir."

"You've got my name pat enough," growled Womersley. "Let's see...I ought to remember yours, from that inquest. Green! that's it Walter Green. Now there's something wrong, Green! You never went to your work at the Euston Hotel the other night, and you disappeared, without any notice, from the club where you live. I've been looking for you! What've you got to say?"

"I...I got this job, Mr. Womersley," said Green. "It's...it's a better job than waiting, sir, and..."

"People don't get jobs in that way, my lad!" broke in Womersley, his voice getting harder and sharper than ever. "That tale won't do for me! You set off for your evening's work at the Euston Hotel the other night in your usual way, but you never turned up at the hotel. Somebody got hold of you. Now..."

An elderly man, obviously an upper servant, butler, or house-steward, came forward from the inner hall, glancing questioningly at the two strangers on the steps.

"What's this, Green?" he asked, authoritatively. "What do these gentlemen want? What is it?" he went on, addressing himself to Womersley in a somewhat altered tone, after a second look at him. "Do you wish..."

"I suppose you're the butler?" interrupted Womersley. "I'm a police officer...there's my official card. Is Lady Cheale at home?"

"She is not," replied the butler, after glancing at the card which the detective thrust into his hand. "Her ladyship left for London early this morning."

"Is Sir John Cheale at home?" persisted Womersley. "If so..."

"Sir John is not at home either," said the butler. "Sir John is away on business...in the North of England."

"Very well!" said Womersley. "I came here to see Lady Cheale. And I find this young man here...opening the door...a footman. I want him! I spent some time day before yesterday searching for him. When did he come here?"

The butler, a quiet-mannered, old-fashioned person, turned a troubled look on the footman.

"Well, really, this is very unpleasant!" he said. "I...I don't understand it! He has only been here two days, but...her ladyship herself engaged him! In fact, she sent him down here from London, with a note to me, saying that she had engaged him as second footman. I..."

"Second footman or third footman, I want him!" exclaimed Womersley. "He's got to give me a full explanation of his recent movements! You say Lady Cheale sent him down from London...was she in London two days ago, then?"

"Her ladyship was certainly in London two days ago!" replied the butler, with some show of dignity. "I have just told you so!"

"But you said that she left here for London early this morning," retorted Womersley. "Do I understand..."

"Her ladyship returned from London yesterday," said the butler. "She arrived here yesterday evening...late."

"And was off back again first thing!" said Womersley. "Why, now?"

"Really, sir!" expostulated the butler. "I fail to see why..."

"I've given you my card!" exclaimed Womersley. "This is a very serious business. I want this lad...but I also want Lady Cheale! It was Lady Cheale I came to find...that I find this youngster here is accidental. Why did Lady Cheale leave again so hurriedly this morning? you may just as well tell me!"

"I believe it was in consequence of a telegram which came for her just before breakfast," replied the butler, who was obviously much upset by the detective's last words. "She hurried over her breakfast, at any rate, and drove off at once to catch an express at Chester. I hope..."

Womersley walked into the hall, motioning Holaday to follow him.

"Now, look here," he said, with a reassuring nod to the butler, "I don't want to make any bother, or cause any suspicion among the servants, but I must have a talk with this lad Green. Either he talks to me here, or he'll have to go with me to the police station at Chester. He'd better talk here...quietly. Can't you show us into a room?"

The butler turned up the ha...unwillingly.

"I don't understand this!" he muttered. "It's very unpleasant for me...my master and mistress are away, and I scarcely know what to do. However, if you're detectives, and want to talk to this young man..."

He threw open the door and showed them into a small parlor, with the air of a man who must needs receive unwelcome visitors.

"Thank you," said Womersley. "And don't alarm yourself! When I've finished questioning Green I shall be glad to see you again, and perhaps to explain matters more fully, but for the present you'd better leave us alone with him. Now, Green," he continued, turning to the footman when the butler had gone away and closed the door, "you'd better be frank and open with me about this business, for I'll warn you at once that you're in a serious position! Sit down there, the other side of that table, and listen to me. You say Lady Cheale sent you down here, night before last, after engaging you as second footman, in London? Very well...how came you to meet Lady Cheale in London? Now, remember, I know all about your movements the evening on which you failed to turn up at your work at the hotel: that is, I know all about them to a certain point. You left that residential club where you've been living at your usual time, all ready dressed in your waiter's clothes, to go straight to your duties as smoking-room waiter. But you never reached the hotel. Now...why?"

Green had listened to all this with a troubled countenance, his eyes turning attentively from Womersley to

Holaday, and always with deepening suspicion. When the detective's final demand came, he twisted restlessly in his chair.

"It's hard on me, Mr. Womersley," he muttered. "It's uncommon hard! I haven't done anything. I wish her ladyship was here!"

"So do I, my lad!" exclaimed Womersley, heartily. "There's nothing I'd like better and my friend here would like it, too, just as much. We want Lady Cheale! that's what we've come down for. But she's not here and you are. Now, take my advice and tell me what you know, for I'm convinced you know a lot. You were a witness, you know, Green, in that Alfred Jakyn inquest, and I'm pretty certain that it's because you were that you're here at Cheale Court. Come, now, why didn't you go to your work the other evening?"

Green gave his questioner a look that was half-sullen, half-significant.

"Because I met Jennison!" he answered.

Womersley threw a quick glance at Holaday, who, hands in pockets, was lounging against the mantelpiece, behind the footman. But quick as the glance was, it was not quicker than the question which shot itself at the unwilling examinee.

"What did you know of Jennison?"

"Saw him at that inquest," muttered Green.

"Had you seen him since?—before the other evening?"

"Yes...once or twice."

"Where?"

"At the hotel. He came there one night and asked me for some information about Alfred Jakyn. I gave him some...about what happened when Jakyn was in the smoking-room the night of his death. He...I may as well tell you, now I'm started on it, Mr. Womersley...he gave me two or three pounds, and said there'd be more to come."

"I see! And what did you tell Jennison?"

"I told him...to put it short...that when Jakyn came into the smoking-room at about nine-thirty, there was an old gentleman and a youngish lady in there; he was reading and she was writing. Jakyn asked me to get him a drink; I went for it, and left the three there. When I came back, after a few minutes, the lady and gentleman had gone and Jakyn was alone. Afterwards...but I told that at the inquest."

"I know...Jakyn was restless, and you saw him read a bit of paper that he took from his pocket; then he went out. Well? what did Jennison say about this?"

"He asked me if I knew the gentleman and lady; I said I didn't, but they'd been staying in the hotel a day or two, and I could find out. I went to find out, and came back to him and told him who they were."

"Just so! and who were they?"

"Sir John and Lady Cheale!"

Womersley again glanced at Holaday, and the American, towering behind Green, made a significant grimace.

"Oh!" said Womersley. "Very well! Now, we'll go back to the other evening, when Jennison accosted you outside the hotel, as you were about to go to your work. What did he say to you?"

"Reminded me that he'd told me there was more money to come, and said that now was the time! if I'd like to profit by what I knew, I could make a lot. Said I must go with him there and then. I said I couldn't...I was about due at my work. He said, let the work go hang! This was a chance of putting hundreds of pounds, ready money, in one's pocket. So I went with him."

"Where?"

"To a place in Charles Street, close by. Sort of shop that had been turned into a surgery...a doctor's surgery."

"A surgery, eh? Whose surgery? What doctor?"

"Well, that Dr. Syphax was there...I'd seen him before, at the inquest. And Lady Cheale...she was there. I recognized her at once."

"Dr. Syphax and Lady Cheale, eh? Anybody else?"

"Yes. There was a young lady that they called Miss Walker; she was there when I got there; she was with Dr. Syphax and Lady Cheale. They were talking...in a sort of parlour behind the surgery. I made out that Jennison had brought her there, just as he'd brought me."

"No doubt!" observed Womersley drily, and with another glance at Holaday. "I should say he had. Well...what took place? What had they to say to you?"

"Jennison said most of it. The others didn't have much to say. Dr. Syphax scarcely said anything, and Lady Cheale only sort of said yes and no to what Jennison said to her. After I got there, and when Jennison had fastened the street door, so that no patients could get in, he talked to me and this Miss Walker...Chrissie he called her, familiar-like, as if...well, as if what concerned one concerned the other, see?"

"I see! Sharers in a secret, eh, Green? Very well, and what did Jennison say? with, apparently, the tacit consent of Lady Cheale and Dr. Syphax."

"Well, he told me that it was of the very highest importance, most serious importance, that Lady Cheale's name shouldn't get out in connection with the Alfred Jakyn affair. He said that Lady Cheale was absolutely ignorant and innocent of anything relating to that affair, and hadn't the slightest idea as to who poisoned Alfred Jakyn, if he really was poisoned. But she'd known Alfred Jakyn in past years, before he left England, and she'd met him unfortunately on the evening of his death, and had spent half an hour talking to him. The only people, however, said Jennison, who could prove that, were me and Miss Walker. I could prove that Lady Cheale was in the smoking-room at the hotel at the time that Alfred Jakyn was, and that the note I saw him read was probably written by her and slipped into his hand, or dropped near his chair for him to pick up; Miss Walker could prove that Jakyn and Lady Cheale were in the saloon of the place where she was barmaid, from soon after ten to about ten-thirty that evening. Nobody but us could prove those facts, Jennison said, and they'd got me there to have a quiet little talk about it."

"And to make you both an offer, eh?" suggested the detective with a laugh.

"That's about it, Mr. Womersley," agreed the footman. "That's what it came to. Jennison said that if it came to us being questioned, as we might be, we couldn't avoid telling what we knew...they'd force it out of us. But, he said, it was absolutely certain this affair would blow over, or the truth would be got in such a fashion that there'd be no suspicion whatever resting on Lady Cheale, and the really necessary thing at present was to get me and Miss Walker away somewhere, quietly, where nobody could get at us to ask inconvenient questions. And then he came straight to it, and he said that if we'd agree to just clear out for a bit, there and then, Lady Cheale would give us five hundred pounds each."

"Spot cash?" asked Womersley cynically.

"Spot cash! He pulled out the money, Mr. Womersley, Jennison did...bank-notes. He put it on the table...two wads of notes. New ones...Bank of England."

"Tempting!" observed the detective. "And you agreed, eh? Both of you?"

"I agreed, yes; I didn't see why I shouldn't," replied the footman. "I didn't know and I don't know now...that I was doing anything wrong. I didn't know that Lady Cheale had committed any..."

"All right, my lad!" interrupted Womersley. "That's another matter. Well, you took your money...did the girl take hers?"

"Yes, she took it. And, of course, we both promised we wouldn't go back to where we lived...we'd clear out for a bit, there and then. And then came the question of where we were to go, d'ye see, Mr. Womersley? It was then that Lady Cheale began to do a bit of the talking...up to that point she left it nearly all to Jennison. She said, as regarded me, that they wanted a second footman at Cheale Court, and that if I'd go there, she'd give me extra good wages: it would be the very place, she said, for me to lie low in for a while. She told me a bit about it, and I agreed, so she wrote me a note to hand to the butler, and after a little more talk, Jennison walked along to Euston with me and sent me off by the next train to Chester."

"Smart work!" answered Womersley. "With your five hundred pounds in your pocket, of course!"

"Yes!" admitted Green. "And I hope, Mr. Womersley..."

"You don't know where the girl, Chrissie Walker, went?" interrupted the detective.

"I don't, Mr. Womersley, I've no idea," replied Green. "I left her there, with Lady Cheale and Dr. Syphax, when Jennison and I went off to the station. It was all of a hurry at the end...Jennison said I'd just nice time, and no more, to get the evening express, and he rushed me off, got me a ticket, and shoved me into the train. That's...that's all I know, Mr. Womersley. And I do hope..."

Again Womersley waved aside the footman's anxiety and his hopes.

"You didn't hear anything of what was being paid to Jennison?" he asked. "Or where Jennison was going? No?

Well, did you hear anything about where Jennison had gone? where he was living?"

Green gave his questioner a sly smile.

"No, not there!" he answered. "But yesterday, when Lady Cheale was here, I posted some letters for her, and I saw one addressed to Mr. A. Jennings, Great Western Hotel, Paddington. And I should say, Mr. Womersley, that A. Jennings is A. Jennison!"

Chapter 17

Womersley rose from his seat, glanced at his watch, consulted his time-table, and, crossing over to the window, beckoned to Holaday to join him there.

"What do you think of all that?" he asked in an undertone.

"Pretty much what I expected," answered the American. "And I guess we'd better be making tracks for London! Of course, the telegram we've heard about, that Lady Cheale got very early this morning, was from Syphax. That's in consequence of our call on him last night. He's warned her."

"The worst of it is, she's got several hours' start of us," said Womersley. "We can't get back to town before evening, and she'll have been there a couple of hours now...we should pass her going up as we came down. However, we've got something to go on now. And, as you say, we'd better shift. As regards this chap..." He turned and went back to the table. "Now, look here, Green," he continued, "I think you've made a clean breast of it."

"Upon my honor, Mr. Womersley, I've told you everything I know!" protested the footman. "I haven't kept a thing back!"

"Very well," said Womersley. "All the same, I think you'd better clear out of this...you can't stop here after giving Lady Cheale away, you know. Now, will you do what I tell you?"

"Certainly, Mr. Womersley...anything, sir," replied Green. "I don't want to stop here...I've been afraid there was something wrong ever since Jennison bundled me off so sharply. You see, Mr. Womersley, they had me at a disadvantage...they sprang it on me, sudden, and got me before I'd time to think. And there was the money, the five hundred pounds...shoved right under my nose, gentlemen! And what am I to do about that, Mr. Womersley?"

"Take care of it!" answered Womersley, with a grim laugh. "Where is it?" The footman tapped his right side.

"Here, sir, in a body belt," he replied. "At least, there's four hundred and eighty of it, all in notes. I used a bit of it, buying things in Chester yesterday."

"Well, don't use any more," said Womersley. "Now listen...you pack up anything you have here, and come back to London this evening. Go back to that club you live at...I'll come there for you to-morrow morning, if I want you. And don't bother about that money; there's a big reward out for news of Alfred Jakyn, and you'll get more than you have there."

"Thank you, Mr. Womersley, thank you, sir!" exclaimed Green, apparently immensely relieved to find that he was not to be led away in handcuffs. "I'll do exactly what you say. But the butler, sir? perhaps you'll say a word or two?"

"I'll speak to him," assented Womersley. He went outside and found the butler waiting in the hall. "Look here!" he said. "This man Green will have to leave here this afternoon...I've given him strict orders that he's to pack up whatever he has and to come up to town by an evening train...I shall probably want him to-morrow morning. So you mustn't put anything in his way, and if Lady Cheale should return here tonight, or during the night, you can give her my card, and tell her that Green has left by my instructions...she'll understand."

"I hope there's nothing seriously wrong?" said the butler plaintively. "Sir John being away, and her ladyship, too..."

"There's something very seriously wrong!" answered Womersley, "as you'll probably hear in due time. But that's all I want at present." He consulted his time-table again, went back and gave the footman a further instruction, and beckoned Holaday out to the car in which they had ridden over from Chester. "Filled up a hole or two in the net this morning, I think!" he said with a laugh, as they went off. "It was an inspiration, after all, that notion of yours about following up Millie Clover! But what do you make of it?"

"I should like to get hold of that man Jennison," answered Holaday. "Seems to me he's a sort of mainspring in this machinery."

"We'll get hold of the young devil right enough, if he's in England!" affirmed Womersley. "I've never trusted him since I first set eyes on him, but I made the mistake of thinking him more a fool than a knave. We'll be on to his track as soon as we strike London. Now look here...it's now one o'clock. There's an express at two-thirty...that leaves us time for lunch at the station. We're due at Euston about six, and I'm going to wire to a colleague of mine, Kellington, to meet us there. And then we'll just go along to the Great Western Hotel and find out if the Mr. A. Jennings to whom Lady Cheale wrote yesterday is Mr. Albert Jennison."

"Well, I reckon he is," said Holaday. "But I don't suppose we shall find him there. You can bet your stars that if the waiter and the barmaid got five hundred pounds each out of Lady Cheale, Jennison got a lot more and has gone away with it!"

"I don't know!" said Womersley. "Jennison, I think, is probably one of these people who believe that if you want to make yourself scarce, the best thing is to take lodgings next door. They're not far wrong, either! as my experience goes. I once searched London high and low for a man who'd made a disappearance from his family, and found at the end that he'd been living all the time three or four doors from them. No! I think we shall find Jennison at that hotel—that's my impression!"

"What I'd like is to find Lady Cheale," remarked Holaday. "Though we'll not get information out of her as easily as you got it out of the footman fellow."

"Information!" exclaimed Womersley. "Pooh! I think Lady Cheale poisoned Jakyn!" Holaday wagged his head to and fro and smiled in his peculiar fashion.

"Well, I don't go as far as all that," he said. "But I think she knows a lot...a lot that I want to know!"

"I say she poisoned him when they were together in that Cat and Bagpipe," declared Womersley stoutly. "Dropped something in his glass when he wasn't looking. For some reason and purpose of her own, of course. Jennison came to that conclusion when he found out she'd been there, and he's blackmailed her. Clear as crystal, my boy! I see all the whole thing!"

"Good!" said Holaday, with a chuckle. "That simplifies matters...for you. But...I don't!"

Womersley took no notice of his companion's uncertainty. He saw a clear case before him, and was jubilant in consequence.

"Hang those Home Office experts!" he exclaimed. "If only they'd tell me how Jakyn was poisoned...I mean by what...it 'ud be a help that I badly want. They've been messing about, speculating, thinking, and I don't know what, all this time, and never said anything definite. What's the use of being experts if..."

But when the train ran into Euston, and Womersley's colleague, Kellington, met them, there was the very news that Womersley wanted...in part, at any rate.

"Come into the refreshment room a few minutes," said Kellington, when Womersley had introduced Holaday to him. "I've something to tell you: a report from those Home Office experts...it came in this afternoon." He led them into a quiet corner, and when each had got a glass before him, bent over the table. "They've found out how Alfred Jakyn was poisoned!" he whispered. "Fact!—at last! And hang me if I'm not surprised that they never thought of it before!"

"Well?" demanded Womersley.

Kellington smiled, as a man smiles who has a good tale to tell.

"You mayn't remember," he went on, "that when Alfred Jakyn's personal effects were taken off him, after his removal to the mortuary, there was amongst them, found in an outer pocket of his coat, a small tin box."

"Yes, I do!" interrupted Womersley. "Ought to! I took it out myself."

"Well, evidently nobody paid any attention to it at the time," continued Kellington. "And so far as we're informed, the doctors only got hold of it during this last day or two. But they did get hold of it, and they found it contained some pieces of home-made toffee...just ordinary home-made toffee. Six or seven pieces...small lumps, you know, broken up. And they experimented with them, yesterday and this morning. A lump was given to a dog. The dog showed no sign of anything out of the ordinary for exactly forty-five minutes. Then he just laid down and died! Died straight off! Another lump was tried on a cat. Same effect...except that the cat survived five minutes longer. But in each case...instantaneous death, when it did come on. And, of course, that's how Alfred Jakyn got this poison. Home-made toffee! Now then...who gave it to him?"

"The box is no clue," observed Womersley. "I remember it...plain tin."

"No wrapper, no label; nothing on it in the way of lettering," agreed Kellington. "I've seen it...saw it this afternoon."

"What was the poison?" asked Womersley.

"They haven't said if they know; that's all they have said...what I've told you. But I rather gathered," added Kellington, "that though they now know its effects, they're confounded puzzled as to its nature! And...but you know how close they are!"

Womersley nodded and took a reflective pull at the contents of his glass.

"Well," he said. "That's something. Now we'd better tell you what we've been after today, and then consult about a move I want to make tonight. It's like this..." Kellington listened attentively to Womersley's story of his day's doings, and at the end shook his head.

"He'll be off!" he said. "Your friend there's right. Waste of time, my lad, to go on to Paddington. I should go to Brunswick Square...to that doctor's."

"No!" declared Womersley determinedly. "I'm going to the Great Western Hotel. Bet you three drinks he's there! Going there, anyhow...we'll try Syphax later."

The other men saw that he was bent on finding Jennison before doing anything else, and then rose with him. But Holaday tapped him on the arm as they walked out of the refreshment room.

"Look here!" he said. "This Jennison, now? Supposing we find him at that hotel we're going to...what are you going to do with him?"

"There's one thing certain about that, my lad!" replied Womersley. "If I put my hand on him, I shan't take it off again...until I'm satisfied. In other words, I shan't let him go! That's why I wired for Kellington to meet us. If we get Jennison, we stick to him!"

"You'll arrest him?" suggested Holaday.

"Well, we needn't put it into such plain language," said Womersley. "We shall just ask him to come with us...we shall show him that we're so fond of his company that we can't do without it...see? Oh, that'll be all right. Once let me get him, and he won't go out of my sight until he's either given a full satisfactory explanation or been safely locked up!"

"That's about it!" assented Kellington. "Let's hope he's there. He's had time to make a fair start, you know, Womersley!"

"I've a feeling that he'll be there," retorted Womersley. "I've a notion that he selected that particular place for a particular reason. But come on...we'll charter a taxi, and we shall know in a few minutes."

He said little to his companions during the rapid run to Praed Street, but when the cab pulled up at the entrance to the Great Western Hotel, he motioned them to keep their seats.

"You stop here until I've made an inquiry or two," he said as he got out. "I'll come back as soon as I know whether he's still here or if he's left. And then..." He went away with a meaning nod and in a few minutes was back with another.

"Mr. Jennings is here!" he whispered. "Mr. Jennings has been here some days. And at this present moment Mr. Jennings is dining. But he'll be out of the dining-room in a few minutes...so come on!"

He led them into the hotel and along the hall to the neighborhood of the entrance to the coffee-room, where he indicated chairs and lounges set about the walls.

"Now, look here," he said, "we don't want to make any fuss, any scene. You drop into a seat on that side of the door, Kellington, and busy yourself with a newspaper; you curl your long legs in that lounge over there, Holaday, and pretend you don't know either of us. When he comes out, I'll accost him; then you stroll up, Holaday, and when I suggest the smoking-room, you come after us, Kellington, see?"

"Suppose he shows fight?" suggested Kellington. "What then?"

"Fight? He?" sneered Womersley. "You mean flight, more likely! There'll be neither flight nor fight, my boy! My impression is that he'll wilt up like a flower under frost! And now, keep your eyes open."

Some minutes went by. People began to come out of the dining-room...men, women.

And suddenly, alone, Jennison came out. He was in his smartest attire; he was apparently very much at home, very much at his ease, and as he passed through the door he was fingering a gold-tipped cigarette. And as he paused in the hall to draw a match from an obviously brand-new solid silver match-box, Womersley, stealing up from behind, tapped his elbow.

"Evening, Mr. Jennison!" he said. "Glad to find you! Perhaps you'll make it convenient to take your after-dinner smoke with me and my friend, Mr. Holaday, of New York, in a quiet corner of the smoking-room? More private there, Mr. Jennison! we don't want to make a scene here."

Holaday had come up by that time, and at sight of his tall figure and of Womersley's threatening eyes, Jennison paled and trembled, and looked as if he were going to fulfil the detective's prophecy. He dropped his match, stooped, picked it up, and in that action gained a little courage.

"What...what do you want?" he demanded, with some show of bravado. "What business have you coming here."

"Now be careful, my lad!" said Womersley. "And be polite or you'll be outside and on your way elsewhere in two shakes. Come on into that smoking-room, now...here's another friend of mine who's dying to make your acquaintance...Detective-Sergeant Kellington, of the Yard."

Jennison gave in. He glanced from one man to the other, and turned towards the smoking-room. There were several men in it already, lighting cigars or pipes, and he bent hurriedly towards Womersley.

"For God's sake, don't let anybody here know what you're after!" he whispered. "There are men here...gentlemen..who know me."

"As Mr. Jennings, of course!" sneered Womersley. "Don't be alarmed, my lad! Here, we're friends of yours, called in to see you. Order coffee and cigars, if you like and we'll make a little party round the table in that nice cozy corner. And you can sit in the corner, and we'll sit between you and the way out! we're so glad to see you, d'you see, Mr. Jennings, that we can't run the risk of your slipping away from us!"

Jennison mechanically took the seat which Womersley pointed out, and summoning a waiter, ordered him to bring coffee and cigars for four. He managed to control his voice, and to show something of a front until the waiter had gone, but his hands were shaking and there was sweat on his forehead when Womersley, who sat opposite to him, leaned across the little table and spoke pointedly.

"Now, my lad," said Womersley, "you listen to me! We've got you, fair and square, and there's no getting away from us. And I'll throw one card out of my hand straight down before you—and you can take a good stare at it. Listen! We've just come from Cheale Court, from seeing Green, the waiter, and Green's made a clean breast of everything he knows. And now you'd better do the same!"

Chapter 18

It was well for Jennison that the waiter just then came back with the cigars, and that Womersley motioned him to wait until the coffee had been brought; the delay gave him time to think. But think as hard as he might, he could see no way of evading the ordeal before him, and he was still upset and thrown out of his balance by the detective's sudden descent. His fingers trembled as he cut off the end of his cigar; his hand shook as he lifted it to his lips. And Womersley recognised his nervousness, and knowing that a nervous man is useless at a crisis, spoke again, reassuringly.

"Take your time, my lad!" he said. "No hurry! but it'll pay you to be candid as candid as Green's been. If you want a word of advice from me...out with everything!"

Jennison waited until the coffee had been set before them, then he glanced at Womersley and ventured a question.

"What...what did Green tell you?" he asked. "If I knew..."

"And I don't mind telling you," broke in Womersley. "This!" He gave his captive a hasty outline of the waiter's story, watching its effect on him. "Now, what do you say to that, Jennison?" he asked. "Anything to contradict in it?"

"No!" replied Jennison. "That's all true. But if I did act in that matter, it was all on behalf of Lady Cheale. Lady Cheale's at the bottom of everything! I...I was only an agent."

Womersley signed to his two companions to listen attentively, and bent across the table to Jennison.

"Now look here, my lad," he said, "you're in a devil of a hole, and it rests with yourself to get out of it. The best thing you can do is to make a clean breast of everything, as Green's done. You've been up to some underhand business all through this affair, you know, and I've been on your track for days, and found out a good deal about you that you'd be surprised to hear of. Now, you answer a question or two, Jennison...it'll be to your advantage. How did you get to connect Lady Cheale with that Cartwright Gardens business?"

Jennison was beginning to think more clearly; he was beginning to wonder, too, if he couldn't rush the situation, bad as it was, to his own advantage. He had gathered the fact that the big lanky fellow who sat at his right elbow was a New York man, and putting two and two together he concluded that he was the representative of the Western Lands people and had five thousand pounds to give away. There might be a chance, yet! and he suddenly glanced at Womersley with the alertness of a man who had taken a decision.

"I picked up a scrap of paper, on the spot where Jakyn died, with her handwriting on it!" he answered.

"How did you know that?" demanded Womersley. "You weren't familiar with the writing!"

"No! But just afterwards I learned from Chrissie Walker, the barmaid at the Cat and Bagpipe, that Jakyn, whom she recognized from the photograph in the papers, had been in there with a lady on the evening of his death...from ten to ten-thirty. That gave me an idea, and I went to the Euston Hotel, compared my bit of paper with the hotel paper, and saw they were identical. Then I found out from Green that a lady had been writing in the smoking-room when Jakyn went in there, and I came to the conclusion that it was she who'd written the note I'd found, making an appointment with Jakyn at the corner of Endsleigh Gardens, close by the Cat and Bagpipe. Then I got Green to find out, from the hotel register, and from the head waiter, who this lady was, and I found she was Lady Cheale."

"Well?"

"I went down there to see her, and told her what I knew...that she'd been with Alfred Jakyn at the Cat and Bagpipe."

"Well?"

"She...she offered me something..."

"Better say money, straight out, Jennison!"

"Well, money, then...to keep quiet about it. I gathered she had strong reasons for not wishing it to be known that she'd met Alfred Jakyn...she knew him at all...very strong reasons."

"Did she give you any idea of what they were?"

"No! Neither then nor at any time! I don't know what they were. I don't know anything, beyond what I'm telling you."

"Did she give you the money?"

"Yes!"

"Where?"

"At a restaurant...a sort of swell tea-room...in Chester."

"Well, you may as well tell us how much, Jennison?"

"It was a thousand pounds...in bank-notes. I was to go to Italy with it, and she was to send me another thousand there, to Rome, when I'd settled down there."

"And you didn't go, of course?"

"I should have gone. But when I got back to town, or, rather on the way, I saw the announcement of the Western Lands reward, and so I wrote to her, enclosing a cutting of it. She...she came up here next day to see me."

"Because, no doubt, you'd told her in your letter that you wanted more!" observed Womersley. "Come, now?"

"I didn't see why I should be a loser!" answered Jennison sullenly. "These people were offering more..."

"Well...go on, and never mind that. She came, you say. Did she give you more?"

"No! She arranged a meeting for next day. But I followed her; I wanted to know where she was going. I followed her to Charles Street, near Euston. She went into a place there that I found was a surgery for very poor people...a six penny surgery. I looked through the window and saw her and Dr. Syphax in an inner room. So I walked in."

"To let her see that you meant business, eh?"

"I wanted her to know that I considered the affair more serious than she admitted, perhaps. But I shouldn't have gone in if I hadn't seen Syphax there. Besides, I knew something about Syphax."

"What did you know?"

"Well, there's a newspaper reporter, Trusford, the fellow you gave that photograph to, after the inquest proceedings, who's on the search in this case. I met him near here one morning, and went with him to see a taxi-cab driver called Shino, who told us that on the night of Jakyn's death he drove a man resembling Jakyn and another man resembling Syphax from the corner of Charles Street and Seymour Street to

Crowndale Road. He waited for them at the Cobden Statue, and drove them back to where he'd picked them up. The Syphax man went away along Charles Street; the Jakyn man towards the Euston Road."

"What time was that?"

"All around eleven o'clock."

"How long did the man wait for them at the Cobden Statue?"

"Inside half an hour, anyway."

"We must see into that! Well, you walked in on Syphax and Lady Cheale. What took place then?"

"I told her straight out I'd followed her because I didn't trust her, and I was certain that she was concealing more than she'd told me of. There was a bit of an angry discussion between me and Syphax. He said it was quite true that Lady Cheale wanted to keep her name out of this Jakyn affair, but she knew nothing whatever as to the cause of Jakyn's death...nothing!"

"Said it as if he meant it?"

"I'm sure he meant it. He spoke most positively. He said that neither Lady Cheale nor he himself had the ghost of an idea as to how Alfred Jakyn came by his death, though they both knew him, and had both seen him that night, but there were the very strongest, gravest reasons why Lady Cheale's name should not be brought in, and it must be kept out at any cost...any cost."

"That, no doubt, suited you! Well and what then?"

"We all three had a talk, and a long talk. Syphax said that it was all very well making it worth my while to hold my tongue, but there were two other people whose silence was just as important as mine...Green and Chrissie Walker and they would have to be got hold of. And...well, I offered to get hold of them."

"Just so, Jennison! And you did...next day?"

"Yes. Next day. I knew Chrissie Walker's habits pretty well...I knew that she went out of an afternoon and returned to the Cat and Bagpipe about five-thirty, so I watched for her, and met her, and talked her round, and took her to Syphax's place in Charles Street. Then..."

"Half a minute! Did Chrissie Walker tell you that she'd just been to the neighboring police station?"

Jennison started. And Womersley knew at once that Miss Walker had not told. Jennison's start and his stare indicated complete surprise and chagrin.

"Been to the police station? that afternoon?" he exclaimed. "No! Had she?"

"Never mind!" said Womersley. "Go on! Then, I suppose, you went to waylay Green?"

"Yes."

"And took him to the same place. Very well...we know most of the rest. But now, where is this girl...Chrissie Walker?"

"She went away north, that night, very late...I believe to some friends in Northumberland."

"With her money in her pocket?"

"Yes."

"You paid Green, and I suppose you paid her? Well...who furnished you with the money?"

"Lady Cheale. She brought it in bank-notes."

"Just so! And...your share? What were you to have?" Jennison hesitated.

"Come now, out with it!" said Womersley. "You may as well!"

"Well, I was to have what I'd already got made up to what the Western Lands was offering," admitted Jennison.

"Was to have! Haven't you got it?"

"No! I was to meet Lady Cheale about it tomorrow morning."

"I hope you will meet Lady Cheale to-morrow," said Womersley, with a grim smile at his two assistants. "I hope to see you both...face to face. But now, Jennison, as Lady Cheale is, evidently, in London, do you know where she is?"

"No! She's not at the Euston Hotel, though; I know that."

"Where were you to meet her tomorrow?"

"Here in Paddington...at a confectioner's in Spring Street."

"You've no idea where she is tonight?"

"I haven't. But..."

"Well, what?"

"She seems to be very confidential with Syphax," said Jennison.

"Very good! Now then, Jennison, you've done right in

making a clean breast, but I want you to give me an absolutely truthful answer to a direct question. Out of all this, have you learned anything really definite...do you know anything definite...as to who poisoned Alfred Jakyn?"

But Jennison shook his head in emphatic and unqualified denial.

"No!" he said. "I know nothing! Absolutely nothing! I haven't even an idea!"

"You never heard anything that made you suspect either of these two...Dr. Syphax and Lady Cheale?" suggested Womersley.

"From them, no!" replied Jennison. He had been gaining confidence during Womersley's examination of him, and he was now disposed to talk, and talk freely. "I never heard either of them say anything that would have made me, or anybody, suspect them of actually poisoning Jakyn. Still, I'd my own ideas, you know."

"Well, let's hear a few of them," said Womersley. "What were they?"

"Well, there's no doubt that Lady Cheale was alone with Jakyn in the saloon at the Cat and Bagpipe," answered Jennison. "She'd an opportunity there, I should think, of putting something into what he was drinking...whiskey and soda, that was, so the barmaid said. He'd two whiskies and soda there. And I know there was an opportunity, because I questioned Chrissie Walker closely about what happened. While they were there, Jakyn left Lady Cheale for a minute or two in the alcove in which they were sitting and went to the counter to buy a cigar. Lady Cheale had a chance then of dropping something in his glass."

"Well?" said Womersley. "And what other ideas?—about Syphax, for instance?"

"Well, there's no doubt Alfred Jakyn was in Syphax's company late that evening," said Jennison. "I don't think there's the least doubt that the men who were driven by the taxi-cab man, Shino, from Charles Street corner to the Cobden Statue were Syphax and Jakyn. Syphax may have poisoned him."

"But still you don't know anything that you can call definite?" said Womersley. "What you really know is that for some reason or other which you can't account for, Lady Cheale was desperately anxious that her name shouldn't come out. That's all?"

"That's all...yes," agreed Jennison. "Silence! that's what she wants. Willing to pay anything for it, too!"

"What part did Syphax take in these proceedings at Charles Street?" inquired Womersley.

"Next to none! My opinion," said Jennison, "is that he was mad...angry at being mixed up in it. I don't think he liked Lady Cheale being there, or bringing the rest of us there. It struck me she'd sort of thrown herself on his mercy. Now and then he said to her that all this was for her to decide...he seemed as if he wanted to wash his hands of it."

"Didn't do much talking, eh?" suggested Womersley.

"He did none about any actual arrangements," replied Jennison. "He seemed impatient, restless...as if he wanted to clear us all out."

"Did you gather that he and Lady Cheale seemed to know each other pretty well? as if they were old friends or acquaintances?"

"They seemed to know each other well enough," answered Jennison. "Every now and then, when she was talking to me, or to the others, she appealed to Syphax. It was then...on such occasions...that he replied as I've told you...that she must decide for herself."

"Did you ever hear either of them mention Sir John Cheale?"

"Sir John? No! except that when I first saw her at Cheale Court, she told me to leave Sir John's name out of it."

Womersley glanced at his two companions, and rising, beckoned them aside.

"He knows nothing!" he muttered, nodding towards Jennison. "Nothing definite! But these other two do...the woman and the doctor. We must get on to them. We don't know where she is, of course. May have gone back to Chester. But Syphax—hallo, what's this?" A waiter had come into the room and was speaking to Jennison. Jennison listened, rose, and approached Womersley.

"I'm wanted on the telephone," he said. "I...I can't think who it can be...unless it's...her! Can I go?"

"With me!" said Womersley. "Come on, where is it?" He walked with Jennison to the telephone and stood by his side. A moment later, Jennison turned a surprised face on him.

"It's Trusford!" he said. "That reporter I told you about. He wants me to meet him at once at the corner of Charles Street...got something important! What shall I say?"

Chapter 19

"Say you're coming!" commanded Womersley. "Sharp now! That'll do...ring off, and come along." He led Jennison back to the door of the smoking-room, and called Kellington and Holaday into the corridor. "Here's another development," he whispered when they joined him. "That young reporter, Trusford, wanted Jennison to meet him at the corner of Charles Street. We'll all go...seems to me that things are going to develop in that neighborhood. Now, look here, young man!" he continued, when they had left the hotel and packed themselves into a taxi-cab. "You listen to me! Not a word to this newspaper chap as to how we came to be in your company, d'ye hear? You'll just say to him that we did happen to be with you when his telephone call came, and that you'd judged it advisable to tell us, in secret, about him and the man Shino, and what you heard from Shino. And...you can leave the rest to me!"

Trusford, loafing about at the corner of Charles Street, stared at the sight of Jennison's companions. Womersley, of course, he knew, and he looked somewhat glum at seeing him, and not over pleased at Jennison's explanation. But Womersley was quick to pacify him.

"We shan't interfere with your job, my lad!" he said reassuringly. "I know you haven't made all this into a newspaper story yet...it hasn't been in your paper, anyway, and we shan't do anything to spoil it. But you work with me...it'll pay you. Play into my hands, and I'll play into yours, d'ye see? And what's the game now?"

Trusford pointed to Jennison.

"He's told you about the taxi-driver...this chap who calls himself Shino?" he said. "And about what he told us...at the mews? Well, I've purposely kept all that back until I could come across the tall man in black clothes and a white muffler who got into Shino's cab with another man on the night Alfred

Jakyn died. Seemed to me, you know, Womersley, that he was some man who lived hereabouts—anyway, that as he'd been seen here once, he'd be seen here again. So I've been looking round this spot at nights. And tonight I'd a piece of rare luck. I was talking to Shino himself at that cab rank round the corner when he suddenly nudged my elbow. "Here's the very man himself!" he exclaimed. I looked round and saw the man he'd described coming along under the gas lamps, walking very rapidly. He passed close by us, and, of course, I knew him in an instant!"

"Knew him, eh?" said Womersley. "Who is he, then?"

"Dr. Syphax! I saw him at the inquest, you know. No mistaking him! Queer looking beggar at any time!"

"Well? What did you do?"

"Followed him! Down Seymour Street and into Euston Road. He walked along there, very fast...he's a peculiar walk, with long strides...until he passed the end of Ossulston Street. There he suddenly met a lady who was coming from the opposite direction."

"Get a view of her?"

"As well as I could. They both stopped, and stood back from the traffic on the sidewalk, talking quickly. She was very much wrapped up about her head and face, but she looked to me to be a pretty, youngish woman, dark...I'm sure she was dark...dark eyes and hair. Very well dressed—furs, and that sort of thing."

"Lady Cheale!" whispered Jennison in the detective's ear.

But Womersley was watching the reporter.

"Well?" he said. "What happened?"

"They stood there for a few minutes...two or three minutes...talking. Then they turned back the way she'd come, towards St. Pancras Station. I followed. They went into the Midland Grand Hotel. And I followed them in there. They turned into the lounge and sat in a corner. I turned in, too, and sat in another...to watch."

"See anything worth watching?" asked the detective.

"I saw them in close conversation. They appeared to be arguing, or debating. He did most of it: she listened, mostly. They talked like that for ten minutes at least; then they seemed to come to some conclusion or agreement, and they got up and went out into the hall. I'd ordered a drink, just to make an excuse for being in there, and I finished it off and went after them. I saw them part: he made for the entrance, and she went to the lift. I concluded, from that, that she was staying there."

"Useful to know that!" muttered Womersley. "But...what after that, if anything?"

"I followed him out. He turned in the direction he'd come, but instead of going along Euston Road, he went up Ossulston Street. I followed him to Charles Street. He went into a sort of shop, and I sauntered by it and found it was one of these cheap surgeries...a six penny surgery, as a matter of fact. There were some people...poorly clad people...hanging about, evidently waiting to see him, and they followed him in. I came to the conclusion that he'd be occupied for some time there, so I made for the nearest telephone box and rang up Jennison...I knew where he was, because I saw him going into his hotel the other day."

"And why did you want Jennison?" asked Womersley.

"Well, I knew he knew something about this Dr. Syphax, through having lived close by him and seeing him at the inquest, and so on," answered Trusford. "And I wanted to ask him if he knew anything about this six penny surgery. Ever hear of it, Jennison?"

But the detective cut in again before Jennison could answer this direct question. He motioned his companions round the corner into Charles Street, keeping Jennison at his side.

"Look here!" he said. "We'll take a look at this place. Come on, now and let's separate and walk on different sides of the street. You, Trusford, and you, Jennison, keep with me...you other two go across. We'll see if Dr. Syphax is still there."

They went along the street in silence, until they came to the place which, in Womersley's opinion, was probably the centrepoint of the Alfred Jakyn mystery. The houses thereabouts were poor, squalid, badly-lighted, but he made out from the glow of the nearest gas lamp that the six penny surgery had originally been no more than a lock-up shop, with a room behind it, and that its present occupant had spent nothing on improving its outward appearance; all that had been done, in fact, was to cover the lower half of the window with cheap paint, and the upper with equally cheap blinds. And behind paint and blinds there was just then no light: the place was in darkness.

"Gone!" muttered Womersley. "Nobody here! And yet, it's not his time for closing. However..."

He went up to the door and tried it. A woman, standing at a door close by, called to him.

"The doctor's gone!" she said. "Went five minutes since."

"Which way?" asked the detective quickly.

The woman pointed towards St. Pancras.

"He went along there," she answered. "He shut up early tonight."

"That's a bother! Nuisance when a doctor's wanted and you can't find him. Let's see, misses...what's his name?"

But the woman shook her head.

"Don't know his name at all," she said listlessly. "He hasn't come here so very long. There was another before him: I never heard his name, either. He was a shilling. This one's a six penny."

Womersley shepherded Jennison and Trusford across the street.

"Drawn blank!" he said, as they rejoined Kellington and Holaday. "Gone in that direction. He may have gone back to the Midland Hotel. Anyway, that's where we'll go. But look here, now; it won't do for all of us to go in there; at least, not all together. We'll break up. This way...when we get there, you, Kellington, go with Jennison into the smoking-room; you go with them, Trusford, if you like. Holaday and I will follow a bit later, but we shall go to the office, to make inquiries. I'll let you know if anything materializes and look here," he continued, drawing Kellington aside and whispering. "Don't you let Jennison out of your sight for a second, on no excuse whatever! Keep by him...I've no doubt we've got a lot of truth out of him, but I don't trust him for a minute."

"And...after you've seen this woman?" asked Kellington. "What're we to do with him then?"

"That depends," replied Womersley. "Let's hear what she's got to say, first. But we're not going to lose sight of him, anyway. He's got that money she gave him, and if he's once out of our hands, he'll be off. So...sit tight by him till I know how things are with her."

Holaday waited in the hall of the hotel while Womersley made inquiries at the office. The detective came to him with a reassuring nod, and taking his arm, led him along a corridor.

"She's here, all right!" he whispered. "What's more, she's staying here under her own name...it struck me she mightn't be. And she's got a private sitting-room, just along here. Now then, we'll knock and walk in on her. Give me your card. There," he went on, putting Holaday's and his own professional card together, "these'll make her jump, I reckon? And now...what're we going to get out of her? For remember, it's Millie Clover that we're about to see!"

"No danger of forgetting that!" said Holaday. "That's what I'm bearing in mind all the time!"

"But at present, it's Lady Cheale," muttered Womersley. "Lady Cheale of Cheale Court, who's been spending money like water to buy silence. And here's her number!" He tapped at the door by which he had paused, and when a woman's voice from within bade him enter, opened it and marched into the room, followed closely by the American. It was a small, brilliantly-lighted room, and Lady Cheale, standing near the fire, at which, as they strode in, she was warming her hands, was in the full glare of the light, and their eyes were quick to see the color fade from her cheek as she turned sharply on them. Her lips parted, and her right hand went up...

"Lady Cheale, I believe?" said Womersley, politely and firmly.

He closed the door behind him and Holaday, and advancing to a center table laid down the two cards with a gesture which invited Lady Cheale to take them up. But Lady Cheale made no offer to touch them; her eyes went to them for an instant, and then straight to Womersley's.

"What...what do you want?" she breathed faintly. "Are you...police?"

"I am, madam," replied Womersley promptly. "You'll see there who I am Detective-Sergeant Womersley of the Criminal Investigation Department. This gentleman is Mr. Holaday, the accredited inquiry agent of the Western Lands Company, of New York. He's charged with the duty of inquiring into the circumstances surrounding the death of Mr. Alfred Jakyn...so am I. And we believe that you can tell us something about that...that's why we're here, Lady Cheale."

Lady Cheale was looking past them...at the door. And Womersley shook his head, as if he had already grasped what was in her mind.

"You'll find it best, Lady Cheale, to have a talk with us," he said. "We don't want to go unpleasant lengths, but..."

"I am alone!" interrupted Lady Cheale. "I've no one to turn to...to seek advice from! Tomorrow morning..."

"No!" said Womersley firmly. "It will have to be tonight, Lady Cheale...just now! Our investigations have gone too far for any further delay. I may as well tell you," he went on, seeing that she still hesitated, "that we were at Cheale Court this morning, and that the young man, Walter Green, has made a full statement as to what went on at Dr. Syphax's surgery in Charles Street the other night. Also, we've got hold of Jennison this evening, and Jennison has made an equally full confession. Now, we want to hear what you have to say. If you'd allow us to sit down..."

Lady Cheale suddenly dropped into a chair at the end of the table, and pointed to others at the opposite end.

"I don't know how Alfred Jakyn came by his death!" she explained. "Before God, I don't! I haven't the faintest idea!"

"That may be, Lady Cheale," said Womersley. "But it's not quite that we want to talk about. In a case of this sort it's necessary to make all sorts of investigations; we've got to find out everything we can about all manner of detail. In this particular case, for instance, I've had to trace Alfred Jakyn's movements as far as I could, and I'm sure you will tell me more about them. We know for a fact, now that Jennison's split..."

"What do you mean by that?" Lady Cheale demanded sharply. "Do you mean that he's told everything about...me?"

"Everything!" retorted Womersley boldly. "All about the Cat and Bagpipe and the barmaid there, and his visit to Cheale Court, and the drugs at the surgery at Charles Street, and the money matters. Now come, Lady Cheale, can't you tell us about your meeting with Alfred Jakyn that night? If you're innocent of his death and I'm not accusing you of guilt, or of complicity, or anything! why not help me to find out how that death came about? Because there's no doubt Alfred Jakyn was poisoned, and the poison must have been given to him that evening by somebody. Why not tell us what you know about Alfred Jakyn?

You met him at the Euston Hotel, didn't you? where you and Sir John were just then staying?"

Lady Cheale sat drumming her fingers on the table. She looked like a woman who is cornered...unexpectedly and scarcely knows which way to turn for escape.

"I met him...saw him there...yes!" she admitted at last.

"Tell us under what circumstances," suggested Womersley.

"I saw him first at dinner," said Lady Cheale. "He came into the dining-room, to dinner, a little late...just before Sir John and I left the room. I recognized him."

"You'd known him before?"

"Years before...yes."

"Am I right in concluding that that was when you were Miss Millie Clover, and in his father's employ?" asked Womersley, eyeing Lady Cheale keenly.

"How do you know I was Millie Clover?" she asked sharply.

"We know that you were, Lady Cheale! We've traced you...pretty thoroughly. We traced you to your old lodgings in Paddington; then to Cheltenham, where you were Mildred Colebrooke, and where, under the last name, you married Sir John Cheale. Was it when you were Mildred Colebrooke or Millie Clover that you knew Alfred Jakyn?"

"It was when I was Millie Clover...at Daniel Jakyn's," Lady Cheale answered, after some hesitation. "Of course, everybody there knew Alfred!"

"And you recognized him again when he came into the dining-room at the hotel that evening? Did he recognize you?"

"I don't think he saw me. Then, at any rate. But later, he came into the smoking-room, where I was writing letters."

"And where your husband was reading a magazine...close by! You contrived to give Alfred Jakyn a note...the note which Jennison found. And in consequence of that note, you later on met him at the end of Endsleigh Gardens, and went with him into the saloon of the Cat and Bagpipe. What was the reason of all that secrecy?"

"My affair!" said Lady Cheale.

"Well, it may be your affair!" retorted Womersley. "But leaving that for a moment, will you tell me this...when you left the Cat and Bagpipe, with Alfred Jakyn, did you go anywhere with him or take him anywhere?"

Lady Cheale hesitated for some time. Then she looked fixedly at her inquisitors.

"If I tell you straight out," she said, "I hope you'll take it as a proof that on that point, at any rate, I'm not keeping anything back. Yes! I did take him somewhere. It was at his own wish. I took him to Dr. Syphax's surgery in Charles Street. And there I left him, with Dr. Syphax!"

Chapter 20

Womersley was beginning to believe in Lady Cheale. Whatever might be her reasons for wishing to bribe Jennison, and the barmaid, and the waiter, he was convinced that she had had no part in the poisoning of Alfred Jakyn. Her wish for silence and secrecy were for something else. That might come out or it might not. But he saw himself approaching an impasse in the matter that he was most concerned about. All this was leading to nothing! The woman before him could tell him a good deal, but not everything; she could take him to a certain point, but no farther. It was with some hesitancy that he tried again.

"You say that it was at his own wish that you took Alfred Jakyn to Charles Street?" he asked. "Did he want to see Dr. Syphax?"

"He knew Dr. Syphax, of course," replied Lady Cheale. "Dr. Syphax is the brother of Mrs. Nicholas Jakyn, Alfred's aunt. Alfred had been to Brunswick Square, hoping to see all the family, but he'd only seen Belyna Jakyn. I told him where he would probably find Dr. Syphax…at a surgery in Charles Street. Dr. Syphax had recently taken over a practice there, among very poor people…he's a benevolent man in his queer way and he was usually there late at night. I showed Alfred where the place was; in fact, I walked there with him. He saw Dr. Syphax inside, and Alfred went in. I returned to my hotel."

"You didn't go in with him, then?"

"I never went in at all. He went in alone. I turned straight back."

"Do you know why he wanted to see Dr. Syphax?"

"No, except that they were related. Of course, a difference had been made by Alfred's return. He was believed to be dead…in fact, I remember that the courts had given leave to presume his death. Naturally, he wanted to see all his relations, and as soon as possible."

"Just so!" agreed Womersley. He was more inclined

than ever to dismiss all thoughts of suspicion as far as Lady Cheale was concerned. Still...she knew things. "I suppose you won't tell me what you and Alfred Jakyn talked about, Lady Cheale?" he suggested, ingratiatingly. "You see our position? the more we know, the better, eh?"

"I'm not going to talk about my private affairs," replied Lady Cheale. "I had my own reasons for seeing Alfred Jakyn privately. I shall not say what we talked about...beyond what I've just told you."

Womersley looked at Holaday and Holaday, without seeming to answer his silent interrogation, leaned across the table towards Lady Cheale.

"There's a question I should like to put to this lady, if she'll be so kind as to consider answering it," he said. "I don't suppose she'll call it of a private nature, either. But it's of the highest importance...to me and my purpose. Did Alfred Jakyn say why he'd come back to this country?"

Lady Cheale looked quickly at her interrogator. And Holaday was as quick in answering her glance.

"That's in confidence!" he said. "I'll go no further and I think I can include our friend Womersley in that?"

"Oh, I shan't say anything!" exclaimed Womersley. "I don't suppose any reply of Lady Cheale will affect what I'm after."

Lady Cheale hesitated a moment.

"Well, he did say something," she answered.

"I'd like to know what?" said Holaday.

"Well...that he was here on a very important financial mission."

"Did he say on whose behalf?"

"No, he didn't. He mentioned no name."

"Did he say..I think he may have said...that his mission was to some of the big men in the financial world?"

"He certainly remarked that he wanted to see some of our very rich men."

"Did you tell him that your husband, Sir John Cheale, was a very rich man?"

"No. He knew that...he knew that Sir John is...well, extremely wealthy."

"Sure!" said Holaday. "Well, now...did Alfred Jakyn ask you if Sir John would be likely to come in at a big deal?"

Lady Cheale started at that question. Her color rose, and she looked at her questioner as if anxious about his good faith.

"I've already said…in confidence," remarked Holaday. "Mine's sure and so's Womersley's. And it's important!"

"No, then, he didn't," replied Lady Cheale. "The fact is, if you want to know, that he'd already told me that Sir John was one of the some half-dozen men in England he wanted to see. He didn't mention any other names…but he did mention Sir John's."

"Was that before or after he knew that you, whom he'd known as Miss Clover, were now Lady Cheale?"

"It was…after. I told him I was Lady Cheale as soon as we met in Endsleigh Gardens."

"And that the gentleman he'd seen you with in the hotel smoking-room was your husband…Sir John Cheale?"

"I forget whether I told him so, in so many words, or not. But he understood it."

"Was it then that he said Sir John was one of the men he wanted to see?"

"Then or soon after."

"Did he express any intention of going to see Sir John at the hotel…where, of course, you were all staying."

Lady Cheale looked confused, and on the way to being distressed.

"I don't like these questions!" she said suddenly. "I don't know what they're leading to! But…yes, he did! He said he'd see Sir John at the hotel next morning."

Holaday gave Womersley a quiet kick under the table at which they were sitting. It was with an equally quiet manner that he put a further question.

"Did you agree to that proposition?"

"No! I asked him not to."

"Why?"

"I had reasons. Sir John is…well, getting on in years. I didn't want him to embark, to get mixed up, in new dealings. He has considerable interests in the United States already, and it's not long since I heard him say he wished he hadn't, as the correspondence relative to them was becoming a bother to him."

"Did Jakyn fall in with your wish?"

"Yes. He said he'd knock Sir John's name off his list."

"Didn't mention any other names that were on it?"

"No...none. And that's all that was said and, if you please, I don't want to be asked any more questions," said Lady Cheale. "I've really told you everything I know..."

"All the same, Lady Cheale," said Womersley, "there are two or three questions that I feel bound to ask before we go. It'll pay you to answer them, I assure you, and to be frank with us. Now, for instance, there's the case of this fellow Jennison...he's downstairs, and practically in the custody of one of our men..we're not going to let him go, anyhow, until we know more. And you can supply this knowledge. Now, did Jennison blackmail you? did he threaten you? He's had money, a considerable amount, from you, and the promise of more. Did he get it by threats?"

"I can't say that he threatened me," answered Lady Cheale, after some consideration. "He came to me with news of this scrap of paper which he'd picked up in Cartwright Gardens. He had it. I saw at once that if he took it to you, my name would come out. Of course, I saw that he wanted to profit by what he'd discovered...I saw, too, that he was a man who might be dangerous. I found out that he wanted to leave his employment in the City, and to have means by which he could travel...so I offered to find him the means."

"He didn't threaten what he'd do, if you didn't?" suggested Womersley.

"I can't say that he did...definitely. He may have implied it...I suppose he did imply it. But what I gave him was voluntarily given."

"Have you given him anything since?" asked Womersley.

"No! I was going to, though...a final payment."

"And those others...the waiter and the girl?' Was that forced out of you?"

"No...it was my own suggestion. I felt that as long as they weren't..well, bought off...I shouldn't be safe. Jennison only acted as a go-between."

"Jennison's given an account of that, Lady Cheale," remarked Womersley. "And he says that these negotiations at the Charles Street surgery took place in Dr. Syphax's presence, and that Dr. Syphax seemed to think you were foolish in carrying them through. Now, why did Dr. Syphax..."

Before the detective could say more, the door of Lady Cheale's sitting-room was opened suddenly, and, without preface or ceremony, the man he was talking of strode in. He threw the door to behind him, and made a curious motion of his hand towards the three people at the table.

"I saw that fellow Jennison downstairs in company with one of your Scotland Yard men, and I guessed that you were here, Womersley!" he exclaimed. "Digging deeper into things...digging deeper, of course!" He dropped into a chair, gave a harsh, sardonic laugh, and leaned towards Lady Cheale, who was watching him with startled eyes. "Told you...told you...told you!" he said, spreading out both hands. "Sure to come out...dead sure to come out. Better have spoken...at once! These fellows...persistent!"

Womersley realized that they were getting to a critical point. He looked inquiringly at Syphax, and Syphax, with another laugh, unwound the white wrapper from his neck, threw it on the table before him, and leaning back in his chair thrust his long hands in his pockets, his whole attitude suggesting that as far as he was concerned he was there to talk.

"And what is it that's sure to come out, doctor?" asked Womersley. "We shall be much obliged to you if you'll tell us?"

Syphax looked fixedly at the detective for a moment, during which his odd mouth and jaw were firmly set. Suddenly he released both...to snap out a question.

"What do you know?"

"Just about this much," answered Womersley, and ran briefly over the various points of information. "There's a lot in that, you know, doctor, that's very suspicious," he concluded, "but I think you could add to it. And don't forget and I hope Lady Cheale won't forget, either...we've got to a stage at which we can't stop. Lady Cheale's been very candid and straightforward with us, though, as a matter of fact, she hasn't told us much that we didn't know already, but she tells us plainly that she has a secret relative to this Alfred Jakyn affair...a secret of such importance that she's been willing to pay considerable sums of money to keep it still a secret. Well, I'm afraid we'll have to know what that secret is! If Lady Cheale won't tell us..."

Syphax suddenly drew one of his hands from his pocket and brought it down with a heavy thump on the table. He turned to Lady Cheale, thrusting out his chin, and jerked out three words.

"My advice! Tell!"

"No!" said Lady Cheale.

Syphax turned to the two men on the other side of the table, screwing up his lips and shaking his head.

"Woman!" he exclaimed sneeringly. "Woman! Illogical! Unreasoning! The feminine! Can't see two inches ahead! Foolish!"

Holaday took a hand, glancing at Lady Cheale.

"I'd just like to remind Lady Cheale that fellow downstairs, and the waiter, and the barmaid, already know a lot," he said. "Does she think that her secret's safe..."

Lady Cheale gave him a sharp look.

"They don't know my secret!" she retorted. "Nobody knows!"

"They know there is a secret," persisted Holaday, "and we know there's a secret."

"And that it has to do with Alfred Jakyn," broke in Womersley. "And, Lady Cheale, you've forgotten that we can investigate. I don't know what my friend here thinks, but my impression is that you knew Alfred Jakyn pretty well in the old days, when you were..."

"Millie Clover!" muttered Holaday. "Didn't I always say from the first that the clue to this business..."

"He did say that," interrupted Womersley. "He suggested the Millie Clover idea as soon as he ran into me! And we can go right back to the Millie Clover days, Lady Cheale, and find out..."

Lady Cheale was rising from her chair. Her glance went towards a door in the rear of the room. But Womersley rose, too.

"No, Lady Cheale!" he said peremptorily. "We can't have that! After all we've learned, I can't let you out of my sight until..."

Once more Syphax smote the table.

"Again I say...tell!" he exclaimed. "Tell! and be done with it! These fellows...sure to get at it! Why wait?"

Holaday made a polite wave of his hand towards Lady Cheale's chair.

"If Lady Cheale would just sit down again," he said

suavely, "I think I could settle this business quite pleasantly. Come, now, Lady Cheale," he went on as she unwillingly came back to the table. "Let's drop this Lady Cheale phase and get back to Millie Clover! When Millie Clover left her lodgings in Paddington, very hurriedly one morning, it was to get married, wasn't it?"

Lady Cheale's answer came at last...half audible.

"Yes!"

"Just so!" said Holaday. "Well, I guess the man Millie Clover married was Alfred Jakyn!"

Womersley started in his chair.

"Good heavens!" he muttered. "I'd never thought of that!"

"Been thinking of that all along," said Holaday quietly. "That's correct, I think, isn't it, Lady Cheale? Well, just so! And now I think it's up to Lady Cheale to tell us anything she likes to say. I reckon Dr. Syphax agrees?"

"Agree to anything definite and explicit!" snapped Syphax. "Better so! Haven't I always said it would come out?"

Lady Cheale sat turning her rings over, and remained in that attitude for a minute or two, her downcast eyes apparently studying the stones. But Holaday saw that she wasn't looking at the rings, or, at any rate, didn't see them; her thoughts were elsewhere. And suddenly she looked up and spoke rapidly.

"I did marry Alfred Jakyn!" she said. "It was a hasty, impetuous affair...I didn't think! And it was a failure...a bad failure. We didn't suit each other a bit, and we parted. He went away...I never knew where...I never heard of him until I saw him again at the Euston Hotel. When we separated, I earned my living, as I had done before, first with a City firm, then at Dr. Syphax's, as his secretary. I never told anybody about the marriage...it's only since this business began that I told Dr. Syphax. Then, when I was at Cheltenham, Sir John Cheale wanted to marry me. I hadn't heard of Alfred Jakyn for well over eight years then, so I knew I could marry, and I did marry Sir John. But..." she paused then, and then went on more hurriedly, "but I never told Sir John about the previous marriage! He doesn't know now...I never wanted him to know...he's getting old, and..."

She rose at that and left the room, and that time Womersley made no effort to stop her. He was looking down intently at the table. Suddenly he leaned towards Holaday and whispered one word. "Motive!"

Chapter 21

Syphax caught the whispered word, low as it was, and turned sharply on the two men at the end of the table.

"Motive!" he exclaimed. "Motive! Yes, of course she'd a motive! Her motive was to ensure silence. Wrong way, hers, in my opinion...wrong all through, and I've said so, ever since I knew. But you! what do you mean by your use of that word...motive? You're not attributing..."

"Don't get restive!" interrupted Womersley. "We're not attributing anything to anybody...at present, though I shan't say what we may do, as things develop. It might easily be said that Lady Cheale had a motive for getting rid of Alfred Jakyn. She's confessed that she married him years ago, and naturally she didn't want him to come in contact with the man she's since married. But we aren't charging Lady Cheale with poisoning him; what we're doing is to get all the information we can. He was poisoned..."

Syphax stopped the detective with a wave of his hand, which finally rested in a gesture towards Holaday.

"Look you here, my man!" he said. "I know rather more than you think I do! I've been in communication...for my own sake...with the Home Office about this affair, and I know that this poison which settled Alfred Jakyn was given to him in some home-made sweet stuff which he had in a small box in his pocket. Now, why has this man, your companion, Holaday, come here? To investigate on behalf of an American company which Alfred Jakyn was representing here! That company has publicly declared, through our newspapers, that it believes, suspects, whatever you like to call it, that Alfred Jakyn was got rid of by somebody inimical to its interests. Very good! How do you know, or, rather, why hasn't it entered into your head to wonder if Alfred Jakyn wasn't given that sweet stuff by these inimical people, who, according to your company, Holaday, must have an existence! They may have had an agent, possibly a woman, on the same boat that brought Alfred Jakyn over. Who gave him that sweet stuff? Is it likely that Lady Cheale carried a box of poisoned sweets about with her, on the chance of meeting a man whom, as she'd never heard of him for over ten or eleven years, she firmly believed to be dead? That's utter nonsense! But it's not utter nonsense, considering the suspicions of the Western Lands Company, to suspect that some agent of its enemies, whoever they are, planted them on him! Look deeper, my friends!"

"Can you suggest anything, doctor?" asked Womersley, a little satirically. "We're open to any advice and any hints and any information, too!"

"I suggest that you find out all about Alfred Jakyn's company on the boat he crossed in," said Syphax. "That can be done! And all about his fellow-travelers between Liverpool and London. And where he went, and whom he met, before his arrival in London, and his visit to Bradmore at the old shop."

"I've done a lot of that already, doctor," said Womersley. "I've seen several people who came over with him. I've talked to two gentlemen...thoroughly dependable and, in fact, well-known men with whom he shared a smoking compartment on the journey from Liverpool to Euston. I've found out as a positive fact that on arriving at Euston he went straight into the hotel, registered, and booked his room. He was in his room for some time, and I've got the hour at which he went out. He must have gone straight to Bradmore's, in Holborn. After that I know all his movements until Lady Cheale brought him to the door of your surgery in Charles Street. But after that...there's a certain blank! And...are you disposed to fill it up?"

"Have I shown any sign that I'm not?" demanded Syphax irascibly.

"You didn't come forward at the inquest..." began Womersley.

"Not necessary...not necessary in my opinion!" retorted Syphax.

"In my opinion, it was, then!" said the detective. "We wanted all the evidence we could get. You knew something that you kept to yourself and you were just as reticent when Holaday and I called on you in Brunswick Square the other night. Still..."

"I think Dr. Syphax is going to tell us...now!" said

Holaday quietly.

"Oh, I'll tell you fellows all I know!" exclaimed Syphax abruptly. "It's little! it's not relevant...in my opinion. Alfred Jakyn walked into my Charles Street place as I was thinking of leaving. Of course, I'd known him in the old days, and I recognized him immediately. He told me in a few words why he'd come back. I was just going out...to see a dying man in Crowndale Road. I asked Jakyn to come with me. We walked along the street, got into a taxi at the corner, and rode up as far as the Cobden Statue. We were talking all the time. He said he should see that my sister and her children didn't suffer by his return. He told me he'd met Lady Cheale, and confided to me that he and she, when she was Millie Clover, had married, found it was a mistake, and separated. He asked me what ought to be done...I said then what I've said ever since, that the best thing she could do was to tell Sir John Cheale all about it. Mind you, although I'd known Lady Cheale for some years, this was the first I'd heard about her marriage to Alfred Jakyn. I was astonished and I foresaw trouble, though, of course, as she'd never heard of him for several years, nine or ten, before marrying Sir John, she was within her rights...not liable to any prosecution for bigamy, or anything of that sort, you know..."

"Just so," agreed Womersley. "That, of course, has been quite clear all along. Well, doctor, you went up to Crowndale Road...?"

"We rode to the Cobden Statue, got out there, and I told the taxi-driver to wait so long...half an hour, or twenty minutes, I forget which. Jakyn and I walked along Crowndale Road, still talking of these things. We reached the house at which I had to call. I told him I might be five minutes there, if my patient was dead—longer, if he was still living. He said he'd stroll about. I went in. My patient was still alive, and I was with him rather more than a quarter of an hour. When I went out of the house again, I waited a minute or two. Then he came along the street, swinging his stick and laughing. And now here is a matter which perhaps I ought to have told. I asked him what amused him. He replied, "Oh, nothing! I came across a bit of mystery along there," and said no more. What I thought at the time was that he'd probably dropped into some saloon bar along the street while he was waiting, and had chanced on some man he knew; he knew a lot of people, shady people, in his younger days. He said no more about it, anyway...he at once returned to the subject of Lady Cheale, and what was to be done. We got into the taxi again, and rode down to the end of my street. There we got out and separated. I went back to my surgery; he walked away towards the Euston Road. That was the last I saw of him, and it's all I know!"

Womersley had been listening to all this with mixed feelings. He felt that Syphax was telling the truth, yet he wondered at him for his denseness in not seeing that the truth he told was of importance. He remained silently staring at him...but Holaday started up from his chair with a laugh that seemed to express what Womersley was thinking.

"Well!" he exclaimed, thrusting his hands in his pockets and beginning to pace the side of the room on which he and the detective sat. "Well! I just reckon that's the most important bit of information I've had delivered to me since I first set out on this business! That's fine!"

Syphax stared at him.

"What is?" he growled.

"Why, that!" declared Holaday. "That...about his meeting an old acquaintance! I guess that's just what we want...to fix things!"

Womersley turned a grim smile on their informant.

"And you call that unimportant, irrelevant, unnecessary, do you, doctor?" he said, with an ill-concealed sneer. "If you'd only told me that at the inquest! But do you really mean to say that you didn't think it worth telling?"

"What, that Alfred Jakyn, while waiting for me, met an old acquaintance?" demanded Syphax. "Frankly, no! I knew enough about Alfred Jakyn's past to know that there are precious few saloon bars in this quarter of the town in which he wouldn't meet an old acquaintance! Alfred Jakyn, sir, lived a very wild and riotous life as a youngster, and frequented these places...everybody knew him! My opinion was and is that while waiting for me he dropped into one of his old resorts...there are plenty of 'em, close at hand, and there came across one of his old pot-companions. I saw nothing exceptional in that!"

"Just so!" remarked Womersley dryly. "All the same, we shall be very pleased to find the old acquaintance he mentioned...if we can!"

"Do so…by all means," answered Syphax, spreading his hands. "I dare say that if you carefully map out this quarter and go systematically from one bar-parlor to another, you'll find that Alfred Jakyn was well known in every one of them from twelve to fifteen years ago, and you may light on somebody who saw him in one on the night I'm referring to…there are three or four within a minute's walk of the door into which I turned!"

"Thank you, doctor…we'll try that line," said Womersley cheerfully. "Much obliged to you. And if we want you again…"

"You know where to find me, my lad, at any time!" retorted Syphax. "Brunswick Square is my address, and if I'm not there somebody always is who knows where I am at that moment."

"All right, doctor!" replied Womersley. He turned to the other side of the table. "And…Lady Cheale?" he asked.

Lady Cheale, while listening to what had been going on between Syphax and the detective, had appeared to be doing some thinking on her own account. She gave Womersley a glance which seemed to imply that she wanted no more questioning.

"I shall be here for several days," she said coldly. "Sir John is coming up to town tomorrow, to join me. I shall tell him everything!"

"Best thing your ladyship can do!" said Womersley. He motioned Holaday to follow him, and in the corridor outside turned with a question. "Well," he asked, "what now?"

"We must find the man Jakyn met while he was waiting for the doctor!" answered Holaday. "I attach all the more importance to that because he didn't tell Syphax anything about it."

"Yes, there's that in it," agreed Womersley. "Well, these fellows downstairs! It's getting late, but tomorrow morning we'll try that Crowndale Road notion."

He beckoned Kellington and his charge out of the smoking-room. Trusford, all agog for news, following in their rear, and outside the portico of the hotel, drew Jennison aside. Jennison, still doubtful as to what was coming, stared anxiously at him.

"Look here, young fellow!" said Womersley. "Just you understand this…there'll be no more money coming to you from Lady Cheale...see? That little game's through! She says she gave you what she did, voluntarily, so I won't interfere. But you be careful, young man, or you'll find yourself in a hole...quick! Now, be off!"

He gave Jennison's forearm a warning grip, and, turning away, motioned Kellington and Holaday to follow him in the direction of the Underground station close by. Trusford ran after him.

"I say, Womersley!" he exclaimed. "I've been waiting all this time...haven't you anything for me?"

"Not just now, my lad!" answered the detective nonchalantly. "Some other time. Good-night!"

He moved off without so much as a look, immediately beginning a close conversation with his companion, and the reporter, after an angry glance at their retreating figures, turned back to Jennison.

"That's a nice sort of game to play off on a fellow!" he exclaimed indignantly. "There's Womersley gets out of me what I know, brings me along here, keeps me kicking my heels for three-quarters of an hour while he talks upstairs, and then goes off with as few words as he'd throw to a dog! I thought he'd have at least given me a notion of what he'd been after."

Jennison made no reply for the moment. Ever since Womersley had collared him as he walked out of the dining-room at the Great Western Hotel he had been in a fever of fear. He had felt certain, positively certain, that Womersley would arrest him, or if he didn't actually arrest him, would detain him, and that instead of occupying his luxurious bedroom at the hotel he would have to pass the night at a police station. He was astonished to find himself at liberty, and for a few minutes he reveled in freely breathing the doubtful atmosphere of the Euston Road.

"Rotten, I call it!" grumbled the reporter. "I particularly wanted to know if those fellows found anything fresh when they went upstairs! Of course, you don't know? Did Womersley say anything when he took you aside?"

"Told me...nothing!" replied Jennison. "Here!" he went on, as they came abreast of a tavern at the corner. "Let's do a drink. I'm wanting one after all that! You'll get nothing out of Womersley," he went on, as he and Trusford elbowed each other at the bar. "He's close, he'll tell nothing! What you want to do is…find things out for yourself!"

"What the devil did you bring him along for?" demanded Trusford. "I didn't want him, nor those other chaps either!"

"Couldn't help it," replied Jennison. "They were there…consulting with me, d'ye see? And I thought…well, that we could work together. But it's as I say…Womersley is close! Gets everything out of you what he can, and tells nothing in return."

Trusford looked gloomily into his glass.

"All right!" he said. "He gets no more out of me…unless I please. What's the time? Not ten yet. I was going to have a look round this Crowndale Road, when you fellows came up. It's not too late…come on! Only round at the back here, isn't it?"

"Five minutes walk," agreed Jennison. He set down his empty glass and drew a long breath of satisfaction to think that it was a glass, and not an enameled tin mug such as he'd probably have got in a police cell. "Oh, all right! I don't mind taking a stroll round there with you. Though I don't suppose we'll see or hear anything…"

"You never know," said Trusford. "What is certain is that Shino took Syphax and Jakyn up there, and that they were in or near Crowndale Road some twenty minutes. They were somewhere!"

"No doubt! But there won't be a notice board on the premises to say exactly where!" retorted Jennison. He laughed at his own humor with the forced, artificial laughter of a man who has been unexpectedly released from danger. "But all right! May as well stroll up that way as any other way."

And as he knew the way, he led the way; up Ossulston Street and Charrington Street, and so into a thoroughfare which "looked as commonplace and ordinary," said Trusford, eyeing it with some disappointment, "as ever they make 'em."

"Not the sort of street you'd associate with a highly scientific murder, eh, old man?" he observed. "Neither the romantic, nor the sordid, nor the squalid about it…typically Somers Townish, or Camden Townish, I call it. Still, how do we know these two were in Crowndale Road, after all. There are side-streets…"

They were near the mouth of a side-street just then, and

Trusford paused, looking down its badly-lighted vista. A female figure came out of the door of a house a few yards away; walked rapidly towards them; passed them; went away towards Charrington Street. She was much cloaked and muffled about head and shoulders, but Jennison suddenly clutched the reporter's elbow.

"I know that woman!" he exclaimed. "So ought you to know her. Didn't you see? Mrs. Nicholas Jakyn!"

Chapter 22

Trusford looked down the street from which the cloaked and hooded figure had emerged.

"Mrs. Nicholas Jakyn, eh?" he said reflectively. "Let's see! Some relation of the dead man's, isn't she?"

"His aunt, by marriage," replied Jennison. "Married a brother of old Daniel Jakyn, Alfred Jakyn's father. If Alfred Jakyn hadn't turned up and I understand that the Courts had given leave to presume his death...Mrs. Nicholas Jakyn and her two children would have come in for Daniel Jakyn's money."

"Much?" asked Trusford.

"No end! Awfully wealthy old chap, I'm given to believe," declared Jennison. "Two or three hundred thousand; I've heard that way, at any rate."

"Then...as Alfred Jakyn is dead?" suggested Trusford. "Eh?"

"Just so! I suppose they come in," agreed Jennison. "Unless he was married. May have been married over the other side."

"I should think not!" said the reporter. "His death's well enough known about across there, and his widow would have come forward. Um! Queer complications, old man! This Nicholas Jakyn lot certainly come under suspicion! And now I come to think of it, I saw them at the inquest, and Syphax sat with them."

"Syphax is Mrs. Nicholas Jakyn's brother!" said Jennison. "She was a Miss Syphax."

Trusford let out a whistle, expressive of his growing suspicion. "I say," he exclaimed. "It all looks more than a bit fishy, Jennison! There's no doubt whatever that the two men driven up to the Cobden Statue, at the other end of this road, by Shino, were Alfred Jakyn and Dr. Syphax. Well, they disappeared along this road, and they're away the better part of half an hour. Where did they go? Somewhere about there!

And now, just about the same time of night, we see Mrs. Nicholas Jakyn here! Suspicious, I call it! By the bye, which of those doors did she come out of just now?"

"Can't say," replied Jennison, glancing along the side-street at the corner of which they were talking. "It's so gloomy along there."

"Let's have a look," said Trusford. He walked slowly down the street, and finally stopped in front of a house, the lower part of which was evidently used as a shop. "I think it was this," he went on. "But it's all in darkness. What's that name on the signboard, over the window shutters? Can you make it out?"

Jennison strained his eyes towards the small, badly-painted signboard which hung above the small front window.

"Reegrater...Herbalist...," he announced at last. "Queer name!"

"Well, I think she came out of here," said Trusford. He got close to the old-fashioned wooden shutters and peered through a crack. "No light in the shop," he added, "and none in the house. I'll tell you what, Jennison! I vote we come back here tomorrow morning and nose round a bit; I'm convinced there's something in this. What business has Mrs. Nicholas Jakyn up here, at this time o' night? and in the very locality to which her brother, the doctor, brought Alfred Jakyn! We can't do anything tonight, for everybody hereabouts seems to have gone to bed, but you meet me in the morning, at that corner, and we'll put our wits to work."

"What time?" asked Jennison.

"Say eleven o'clock. That'll suit me," replied Trusford. "I'll be here eleven sharp. Who knows what we mayn't find out!"

Jennison agreed, and presently went off to his hotel...to spend a quiet hour by himself in the smoking-room before he repaired to his bed, and to think, seriously and deeply. In his opinion, he had just cause for deep and serious thought. But it was not of his own escape that he was thinking; by that time he had come to regard that as a matter of course; after all, he said to himself vain-gloriously, what could Womersley have done to him? If Lady Cheale chose to pour her money into his hands, what the devil had Womersley and all the detectives and police in London to do with it? All the same, he knew that Womersley was speaking truth when he said that all that was at an end; that he, Jennison, would get no more out of her ladyship. And it hit him badly. If Womersley hadn't come along, with that lanky American chap at his elbow, he would have been very nicely off next day...very nicely off indeed! All gone now...damn Womersley.

But the reward offered by the Western Lands people! that was still to be got. They couldn't, and he felt sure they wouldn't, go back on their word! Well, there was yet a chance for him to put himself in the position of being able to ask them to make their word good. He already knew much; he had learned more that night. He had not said so to Trusford, but he firmly believed that the seeing of Mrs. Nicholas Jakyn in that Crowndale Road district was the most important bit of evidence he had got so far, and he was determined to follow it up. And he would do it by himself. No sharing! Why should he let Trusford come in? Seriously, he would keep his word and meet the reporter at eleven o'clock next morning...yes! But he would also take care to have been over the ground and to have made his own investigations long before Trusford appeared. First come, first served!

And by ten o'clock on the following morning, Jennison, unobtrusively attired, was in Crowndale Road once more. It was a dull, foggy morning, chill, damp, and his surroundings were anything but inviting. Still, Jennison welcomed the fog; its gray folds served to shroud his movements, and enabled him to examine things without being observed himself. He went straight to the narrow side-street from which he had seen Mrs. Nicholas Jakyn emerge, and to the shop out of which Trusford thought she had come.

There was the queer name, Reegrater; there, in the now unshuttered window, were evidences of the trade carried on within. He stood for a minute or two, peering through the dirty window-panes at the things displayed behind them...bunches of herbs, bottles of queer-looking objects, dried plants, phials of colored stuff, trays of lozenges, all alike dusty and uninviting. But Jennison wasted little time in gazing at these things; his object was to see into the shop beyond. The window, however, was so full of wares that he could see little, and presently, having invented an excuse for entering, he opened the door and walked in.

The shop was empty. It was a small, old-fashioned place, of a piece with the little window. The things that were in the window were in the shop, too, hung about the walls and on the counter. There was a curious odor in the atmosphere, acrid, pungent; it got into his nostrils and made him sniff. But there was no human being behind the counter, though the shop was not without life...a large black cat sat on a tub in a corner, staring balefully at him out of big, yellow eyes. In another corner a hanging clock ticked monotonously.

Jennison knocked once, twice, thrice, on the counter, each time more loudly and insistently. Nobody appeared. The cat remained motionless, staring at him. No sound came from behind a door in the back wall of the shop, a door that had panes of glass in its top panels, and a red stuff curtain across the lower panes. And after a few minutes of waiting and indecision, Jennison went over to this door and looked through the glass.

There was a room beyond, a living-room, half-parlor, half-kitchen. He could see most of it, and, like the shop, it was empty of human life. But there was a fire, a blazing, comfortable fire, on the hearth, that seemed to announce that the owner of the place was somewhere about; upstairs, perhaps, or in the back premises. And presently Jennison opened the door and called loudly: "Hallo!"

His voice sounded curiously ghostly, he thought; it was as if he called where there was no possible chance of reply. Certainly he got none. He called again, and yet again, without result. And at that he pushed the door wide, and walked into the room and looked round.

There was another cat there...a she-cat, blinking on the hearth, benevolently regard-full of a kitten that played about on the rug. Against the wall next to the shop, on a small side-table, were breakfast things...a tea-pot, a cup and saucer, plates, bread, toast, jam, bacon and egg. But Jennison saw at once that whoever it was that had sat there to break his or her fast, had been interrupted, suddenly, and by some urgent business. A knife and fork lay across a scarcely-touched slice of bacon on one plate; a round of dry toast had been just broken into; the cup was three-quarters full of tea; the top had been chipped off the egg, but the egg was uneaten. The very position of the chair showed that its occupant had risen suddenly from it, thrusting it aside, and had not returned to it. Whatever the reason was, the person who had sat down to egg and bacon, toast and tea, had suffered an abrupt breaking-in upon the meal, risen from it, and never come back to it.

By this time Jennison was so sure there was nobody about the place that he began to look round, leisurely. There was a sort of scullery or lobby behind the living-room, and in it an outer door, which stood half-open. He looked out of it into a long, narrow, high-walled passage that ran between houses, and gave, in the distance, on a street, and it immediately struck him that if the owner of the herbalist establishment had found reason to flee suddenly, this was the way by which he or she had gone. He turned from that to the staircase, which ran from the side of the living-room. To make sure that he really had the place to himself, he called up it two or three times. When no answer came, he walked up to a landing.

A bedroom door stood wide, and Jennison crossed its threshold and looked round. The bed was neatly made, but across its coverlet were thrown female garments, tossed down anyway, as if they had been hastily discarded for others. They were the sort of garments that a woman would wear who had house-work to do...a print gown, a linen overall, suchlike. And in a chest of drawers against the wall, drawers were left wide open, as if other garments had been quickly snatched from them, and on the floor a hat-box lay with its lid off and tissue-paper wrappings thrown aside. Clearly, the owner of that house was a woman, and as she sat at her breakfast some message had come to her which made her leave her meal, rush upstairs, change her attire, and flee her own roof as if...as if she were not safe in it for one minute longer!

Jennison wasted no more time in looking round. There were other rooms opening off the landing, but he gave nothing but a glance at their closed doors. Hurrying downstairs, he went into the shop and from its threshold looked out on the street. It was a quiet, dismal street, that; there were few people about. But right opposite was a greengrocer's shop, and the greengrocer himself was at its front, busily engaged in laying out his various wares. And Jennison closed the shop door behind him, and crossed the street. He accosted the greengrocer with a look and tone suggesting confidence and mystery: the greengrocer, ceasing from arranging his roots and fruits, looked over the way.

"Out?" he said. "I'm sure I can't say, mister!" he answered. "I saw her take down her shutters at the usual time...half-past eight. She's perhaps in the back?"

"No!" answered Jennison. "There isn't a soul in the place...unless cats have souls. I've been downstairs and upstairs. There's nobody there."

"Then she must have gone out by the back way," said the greengrocer. "There's a passage at the rear, leading to another street. But...leaving the shop open! Not that there's such a lot of custom," he added, with a chuckle. "People don't buy that sort of dried stuff as they buy this!"

He waved his hand at his own commodities, and Jennison, sizing him up as a man you could talk to freely, became more confidential.

"Look here!" he said. "I may as well tell you I'm a private inquiry agent. I want to know something about that place and its owner. It's a woman, eh?"

"Mrs. Reegrater," said the greengrocer readily. "Elderly woman."

"You know her?"

"Just as you do know neighbors! Know her by sight, and as much as to pass the time of day with her...if I come across her. Quiet, retiring sort of person, she is...does a fair bit of business, I fancy, with working folks about here. They're great believers in these herbalists, you know...believe in them and their stuff more than in doctors or chemists."

"Has she been here long?" demanded Jennison.

"Well, not so long...as things go," said the greengrocer. "Mother of two or three girls, maybe. But it's my belief it's not her business at all. I think it belongs to a lady that you see hereabouts pretty regular, a lady that's generally there of an evening. Comes to take the day's money, I expect."

"What sort of a lady?" asked Jennison. "What's she like?"

"Elderly! Tall, thin woman, very similar in appearance to Mrs. Reegrater; dresses usually in black. I saw her the other night. You can often see her if you're about here...she's generally across there till late...I've often seen her leaving. In fact, it's only at night that you do see her...never see her in the day time, or close to."

"You don't know her name?" suggested Jennison.

"No more than I know yours, mister!" said the greengrocer. "But that's London. You can live next door to a person for twenty years here and know nothing about name or business...unless it's a shop. No! I don't know the lady's name. But, as I said, it's my belief it's her business, and Mrs. Reegrater just manages it."

"Mrs. Reegrater lives alone?" asked Jennison.

"Except for a couple o' cats, and a kitten now and then, yes. Quiet woman, as I said. Keeps herself to herself."

Jennison made no remark on this. He was watching the shop opposite. Presently the greengrocer spoke again.

"Queer that she should go out like that, leaving nobody there!" he said musingly. "But there, she's nobody to leave. And customers don't tumble over each other across there, you know! One now and then...that's how it is."

Jennison was thinking. He had no doubt now that it was to that herbalist's shop that Alfred Jakyn had gone when he came up Crowndale Road. Perhaps he had looked into its window out of mere curiosity while waiting for Syphax, and had seen inside somebody that he recognized; perhaps that somebody had been Mrs. Nicholas Jakyn; perhaps Syphax had purposely brought him there to see Mrs. Nicholas; perhaps... but it was idle to speculate. There were certain things that he now knew as facts and he meant to make good use of them, to his own benefit.

"What time at night does this Mrs. Reegrater shut up shop?" he asked suddenly. "Early or late?"

"Oh, late!" answered the greengrocer. "Known her keep it open till twelve o'clock. Good part of her trade's done at night. That lady I spoke about...she's generally here very late...I've seen her leaving after eleven, many a time. She never leaves though, till after the shop's closed. But what's it all about, mister?"

"I'll tell you later," replied Jennison. "Serious matter...very. I'm just going to see if she's come back."

He went across the street and into the shop, and through the glass-pane door to the parlor. Everything was still as before, but on the hearthrug the kitten was chasing and frolicking with a crumpled ball of pink paper. Something prompted Jennison to pick that ball up and to smooth out the folds. And the next instant he found himself staring at a telegram on which was a message of three words:

"Leave at once."

"And...she left!" muttered Jennison, with a cynical laugh. Didn't stand on the order of her going, as they say. "Oh..." He paused as the clock in the shop began to strike. "By George! eleven!" he exclaimed.

"Trusford..."

Crumbling the telegram in his hand, he hurried out of the room and the house, and made round the corner of the street into Crowndale Road...to run, full tilt, into the arms of Womersley and Holaday.

Chapter 23

Womersley had a grip of Jennison's arm before Jennison had fully realized what he had run into. He slewed him round with a jerk and a stern exclamation.

"Now then," he demanded, "what's up now? what are you after? what are you doing here?"

Jennison twisted himself out of the detective's clutch and sheered off a little.

"You keep your hands to yourself, Womersley!" he answered defiantly. "I'm here on my own business, and I reckon you'd give a good deal to know what it is! Will know what it is, will you? Not till I've had a word or two with him," continued Jennison, pointing to Holaday. "I may tell the two of you, then...but not till then! And you can bluster as much as you like," he went on, as Womersley began to show signs of anger. "I know something, and I'm top dog in this! Show any more of that, and I'm off...elsewhere!"

"Well, now, what is it?" asked Holaday, interposing himself between them. "You want a word or two with me..."

"Come aside!" said Jennison. He retreated a few yards along the street, eyeing Womersley jealously. "Look here!" he went on, as the American came up to him, smiling good-humoredly. "That offer of your company's? the reward, five thousand...does it hold good? Will it be paid?"

"Sure!" answered Holaday. "No doubt of it...if the conditions are fulfilled."

"If I told you something that fulfilled the conditions, you'd see that I got it?" persisted Jennison. "You really would, honest Injun?"

"Honest Injun!" laughed Holaday.

"I'm trusting you!" said Jennison. He turned and beckoned Womersley, imperiously. "Come here, you!" he commanded. "I've got Holaday's word, and now I'll tell you what I've just found out. Now you listen as you've never listened in your lives..."

Jennison's small bit of literary ability helped him to present his story with an eye to dramatic effect. He told his hearers why he had come up to Crowndale Road, what he had seen in the herbalist's shop in the side street, what he had heard from the greengrocer. The more he told the more eagerly the two men listened, and at the end Womersley made a move for the corner.

"Shop still open?" he asked.

"Unless she's come back and locked the door," answered Jennison. "Which isn't likely!"

He led them round to the shop and into it, and into the parlor, and finally upstairs, indicating various things in corroboration of his story. His companions saw for themselves, looked, wondered, surmised. In the bedroom, Womersley, turning over the discarded garments, picked up a lady's handkerchief, and, after a moment's examination of it, held it towards Holaday, pointing to a corner.

"Look at that!" he said.

Holaday looked and started. There, daintily woven into the fabric was a name Isabel Jakyn. He made a sound expressive of surprise.

"Just so!" remarked Womersley. "That's what I feel! And yet...not so surprising after all. Come along downstairs."

He put the handkerchief in his pocket, and led the way back to the street. And once outside the shop door, Jennison, looking round, saw Trusford at the corner, glancing up and down. Womersley, too, saw him, and beckoned.

"Look here," he said, turning to Jennison as the reporter came running up, "you've done a bit of good work this morning, and now you can do more. Stay here, and look after the place while Holaday and I do a bit of investigating. If the woman turns up..."

"She won't!" said Jennison.

"Well, if she does, send Trusford for the nearest policeman, and tell him what's going on, and that I shall be back," continued Womersley. "You can tell Trusford all about it...but no printing or anything yet, mind you! Just give me that telegram...I want to look into that! And now, don't leave that shop till I'm back, or you hear from me."

He put the telegram into his pocket, and, touching

Holaday on the arm, went across the street. The greengrocer stood at his door, keenly interested.

"You've given our friend across there a bit of information," said Womersley, putting his card into the man's hand. "Can you give me a bit more? The shop opposite, you say, is kept by a Mrs. Reegrater, and there's a lady who's very similar to her in appearance, who, you believe, is the real proprietor, and is there of a night, leaving late? Just so! Now, have you ever seen that lady in the daytime?"

"No, never!" replied the greengrocer. "Only at nights, late."

"Have you ever seen her and Mrs. Reegrater together?"

"No, I never have. I've never seen Mrs. Reegrater except for a minute or so, looking out of her shop door. The lady I never saw at any time except late at night."

"When did you see her last?"

"Can't be sure whether it was last night or night before. It's always very late. I'm a late man myself...I often smoke a pipe, strolling up and down, last thing, and that's when I've generally seen her."

"Much obliged to you!" said Womersley.

He motioned Holaday to follow him, gave a glance at the herbalist's shop, inside the door of which Jennison and Trusford were visible in excited conversation, and walked towards the corner. There he drew out the telegram.

"See where that was sent off from?" he asked. "Grenville Street. But you don't know where Grenville Street is, nor what its present significance is! Grenville Street, my boy, is at the bottom of Brunswick Square, close to...Syphax's!"

Holaday whistled.

"To be sure!" said Womersley. "That's it! Now, let's get a taxi and hurry down to the Grenville Street post office. I want to know who sent that telegram to Mrs. Reegrater, and as it's scarcely three hours since it was sent we shall easily find out. Was it Syphax, or was it Mrs. Nicholas Jakyn? For it strikes me, Holaday, that the mysterious lady who comes to that shop of a night, is the doctor's sister, the aunt of Alfred! What do you think? Hallo! there's a taxi yonder. Hi! Yes," he went on, as the cab turned and came along to them, "what do you think?"

Holaday was standing at the edge of the pavement, his arms folded, his eyes cast down, apparently at the toes of his big shoes, his mouth set in a straight line. Suddenly he looked up; his mouth relaxed into an almost seraphic smile, and he laughed, as if an amusing idea had come to him.

"I'll tell you what I think!" he said. "I think that Mrs. Reegrater and Mrs. Nicholas Jakyn are one and the same person! Sure!"

Womersley uttered an exclamation that was half skeptical, half acquiescent.

"Ah, you're thinking that, are you?" he said. "Well, I'm beginning to suspect it. It may be so! But I don't know!"

"I don't think there's any doubt of it," answered Holaday as they settled themselves in the cab. "Put things together. Alfred Jakyn said to Syphax when he rejoined him after strolling around in this Crowndale Road that he'd come across a bit of a mystery. From what we know now, I take it that what he'd come across was his aunt...keeping that herbalist's shop under the name of Reegrater.

"Reconstruct it for yourself...he wanders around while he's waiting for Syphax; he sees a light in the shop window, he goes and peers in, he sees his aunt. He enters. We don't know what happens then, but I guess she gave him that home-made toffee! gave him a lump of it there and then, maybe, with perhaps a jocular reference to the fact that she knew he used to have a sweet tooth. Clever woman, no doubt, this Mrs. Nicholas Jakyn...unscrupulous, too! But...is she identical with Mrs. Reegrater? I think so. That man who sells potatoes and carrots says that he never saw Mrs. Reegrater and the mysterious lady, together. Sometimes he saw one...sometimes another. Now I take it that Mrs. Nicholas Jakyn ran that shop...she was Mrs. Reegrater when she ran it, and she was Mrs. Jakyn when she left it. And from the fact that she'd had her breakfast, or was getting it there this morning, I conclude that occasionally she spent the night there...in fact, I reckon that we've hit on a very good instance of a double life. But we, or you, can find that out; that parlor-maid of Syphax's can tell if Mrs. Nicholas was out o' nights much, and, in fact, a good deal about her habits. And...the daughter knows!"

"Oh, the daughter!" exclaimed Womersley. "She knows a damned lot! Been shielding her mother, of course. Don't you remember what the parlor-maid told me she'd overheard? Well...it's natural for a daughter to shield her mother! But it makes her accessory. I expect it was the daughter sent this telegram. But I'll know that in two minutes when we strike the post office."

"Oh, the daughter sent it!" said Holaday. "Something roused her suspicions this morning that things were at the climax. That's been the way of it and it's given the woman a good two hours' start."

"Start or no start, I'll run her down!" muttered Womersley. He bade Holaday remain in the cab when they reached the Grenville Street post office, hurried in, and within a minute or two was back. "That's settled," he said, with a nod. "The daughter's sent it! Handed it in herself...they know her well enough there. Well...we're close to Syphax's! I'll pay this man, and then . . ."

The house in Brunswick Square looked innocent enough in its high respectability. It was a smart house, seen from outside...brightly polished windows, shining paint and brass, clean blinds and curtains, and well-kept house. And the parlor-maid who presently responded to Womersley's knock looked in keeping with it in her coquettish cap and apron. But the cap wagged vigorously above her glossy hair as she saw who the callers were.

"Not a soul in!" she exclaimed, before Womersley could speak. "All out!"

Womersley stepped across the threshold, motioning Holaday to follow him. He signed to the girl to shut the door.

"Look here," he said in a significant whisper, "what's been going on here this morning? But first...was Mrs. Jakyn in last night?"

The parlor-maid shook her head.

"No! I might have told you before, but I never thought of it. She's often out at night...I've an idea she goes nursing or something. And, of course, she's out all day, as a rule. No...she wasn't here at all last night."

"Well, this morning? What about the doctor and Miss Jakyn? Notice anything about them or hear anything?"

"I heard him talking to her at breakfast, a good deal. Of course, I couldn't catch what it was, but I was in and out of the room, and I heard bits. He seemed to be telling her something about some talk he'd had last night. I heard your name once."

"He's been telling her about the talk at the Midland

Hotel," muttered Womersley in an aside to Holaday. "Well," he continued, turning to the girl, "and after that?"

"Nothing, except that soon after the doctor had gone out...he went out very early this morning...I saw Miss Belyna at the desk in the dining-room writing on a telegram form. She went out with it herself. When she came back she went upstairs and came down again dressed for going out, and she told me that she'd not be in during the morning. Then she went away, and, of course, she's not come back yet."

"Just so!" said Womersley, nudging Holaday's elbow. "You don't know where she went?"

"She turned down towards Guildford Street," replied the girl. "That's all I know. She was walking then, but she might have got a taxi round the corner...she always goes about in taxis when she does go out. Generally, I call one for her...but this morning she didn't tell me to."

"You don't know where Dr. Syphax is?" asked Womersley.

"Gone on his rounds, I expect, but I don't know where. He's generally in by one o'clock," said the parlor-maid.

"We'll likely look in again...about that time," said Womersley. "If any of them come in, don't say we've been here...keep that to yourself." He led Holaday from the house, walked a few yards down the square, and turned to his companion with a cynical laugh.

"Got the start of us...as they usually do, Holaday!" he remarked. "But in this case, it's not a long one, and I think they'll be tracked pretty easily. Now, we'll ring up for help, get Kellington and another or two of our men, and start the hunt! Come along!"

But at the corner Holaday paused. He gave Womersley one of his curious smiles and shook his head.

"Well, you'll excuse me, Womersley!" he said. "I'm through! That's your job...it's not mine. My job's done! I came over on behalf of our company to make sure either that Alfred Jakyn was murdered to prevent him doing our business, or he wasn't! I know now that he wasn't. Alfred Jakyn was murdered by his aunt so that she and her children could come in for the money! I'm satisfied of that and so my work's done! And I'm not going to take any share in hunting women, anyway. Not to my taste!"

"Criminals! One of 'em, anyhow!" exclaimed Womersley. "A murderess!"

"No doubt...but not my job!" said Holaday dryly. "Yours! So I'll tell you good-bye!"

Without as much as a handshake, or the conventional remark that he'd been glad to meet Womersley, Holaday nodded and turned his big shoes in the direction of his hotel; nor, having turned, did he once look round again. For a moment the detective stood, staring after his retreating figure...then, with a muttered exclamation of mingled surprise and amusement, he, too, turned on his heel, and made for the nearest telephone-box.

The End

Printed in Great Britain
by Amazon